OUTER BANKS

# POGUE LIFE

By John B, JJ,
Kiara, Pope, and Sarah
with Joey Elkins

AMULET BOOKS • NEW YORK

PUBLISHER'S NOTE: This is a work of fiction. Names, characters, places, and incidents are either the product of the author's imagination or used fictitiously, and any resemblance to actual persons, living or dead, business establishments, events, or locales is entirely coincidental.

Cataloging-in-Publication Data has been applied for and may be obtained from the Library of Congress.

ISBN 978-1-4197-5933-8



Book design and illustrations by Celina Carvalho

*COURTESY OF PIXABAY:* **Cover:** duct tape, peace sticker. **Throughout:** torn paper, Post-its, transparent/yellow/brown/colored pieces of tape, duct tape. **13:** small notebook pages. **16:** ship illustration. **18–19:** shipwreck photos, and ship illustration. **20:** boat illustration. **23:** boat illustration (*bottom right*). **29:** ship illustration . **31, 33, 38–39, 92–93, 97, 121, 122–23, 134, 149, 157, 161, 167, 180–81:** emojis. **45:** wallets, flip-flops, cigar, charger, pizza. **47:** bonfire photo. **56, 57, 68, 69, 77, 91, 103, 142, 159, 160, 168, 169, 170–71, 176–77, 179, 180–81, 186–87, 187, 188, 190–91, 192, 196, 198–99, 200–01, 205:** sticker illustrations. **55:** surfer girl. **94:** sunglasses, lighter, soap, cigarette, flip-flops, chocolate, glycerin bottle, safety pin, gum. **108:** turtle photos. **111:** Beer glass. **112–13:** sunflower, ukulele. **116:** candles, tarot cards. **117:** hermit crab. **120–123:** sign symbols. **126:** menu illustrations. **128:** shrimp. **136:** pirate skull (*top left*). **142, 152, 154–55, 156, 157, 167:** speech bubbles. **148:** black wasp. **152:** exclamation point. **159:** salmon illustration. **160:** poster. **166:** lobster plate, clam plate, shrimp cocktail. **167:** fish illustrations. **168:** blueprints, graduation gown. **172:** Gameboy, iPod. **173:** Periodic Table. **176–77:** blue flower illustration. **180–81:** stars photograph. **184:** spiderweb. **193:** pink paper. **205:** "Top Secret" folder, stamps. **206:** dolphin. **207:** Hearts and mermaid tattoos. ***COURTESY OF SHUTTERSTOCK*:** **Cover and throughout:** liquid stains, duct tape. **120–21, 122–23:** sign cards. **127:** lemon pie. **189:** waiter's arm. **193:** golf grass photo. ***ALL OTHER IMAGES COURTESY OF NETFLIX.***



Printed and bound in U.S.A.
10 9 8 7 6 5 4 3 2 1

Amulet Books® is a registered trademark of Harry N. Abrams, Inc.

**ABRAMS** The Art of Books
195 Broadway, New York, NY 10007
abramsbooks.com

# SUMMER GOAL:
# GOOD TIMES ALL THE TIME

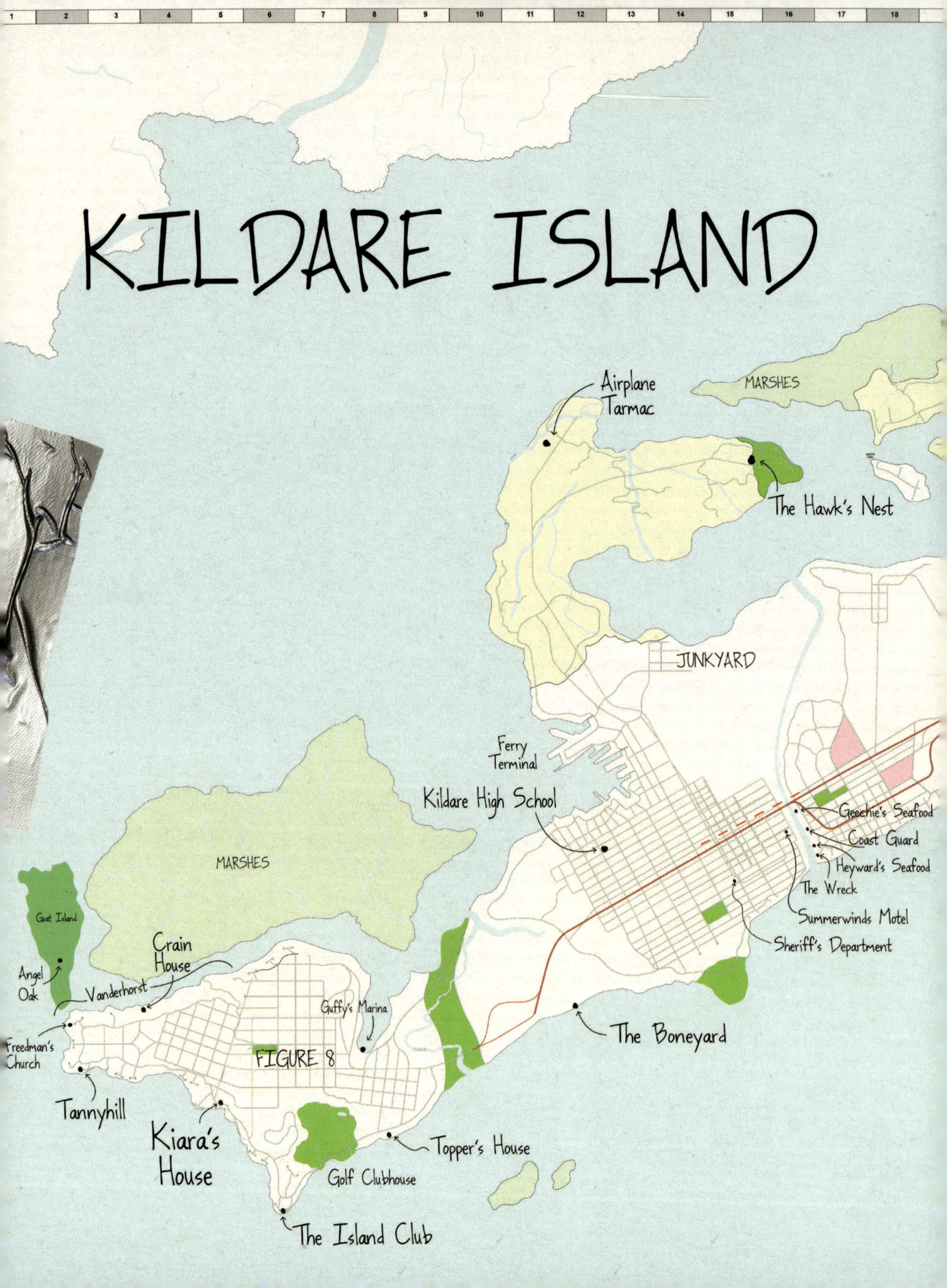

KILDARE ISLAND
Airplane Tarmac
MARSHES
The Hawk's Nest
JUNKYARD
Ferry Terminal
Kildare High School
Geechie's Seafood
Coast Guard
Heyward's Seafood
The Wreck
Summerwinds Motel
Sheriff's Department
MARSHES
Goat Island
Angel Oak
Crain House
Vanderhorst
Freedman's Church
Guffy's Marina
FIGURE 8
The Boneyard
Tannyhill
Kiara's House
Topper's House
Golf Clubhouse
The Island Club

21 22 23 24 25 26 27 28 29 30 31 32 33 34 35 36 37 38
MARSHES
Sunken
Grady White
Barry's Trailer
MARSHES
The
Chateau
THE CUT
JJ's House
MARSHES
Redfield
Lighthouse
The Shoals
Welcome To The
OUTER BANKS
PARADISE ON EARTH

# JOHN B

# WANTED

# $25,000 REWARD

## JOHN B. ROUTLEDGE

Being wanted for a murder I didn't commit really harshed my summer vibes. And only a $25,000 reward? C'mon, I'm worth at least triple that.

JJ, you didn't draw a dick on my forehead. I'm impressed at your restraint.

I really matured this summer. —JJ

**UNLAWFUL FLIGHT TO AVOID PROSECUTION**
**FIRST DEGREE MURDER**

## DESCRIPTION

**FUGITIVE KD-ID:** ............ KDIS88991
**WANTED FOR:** ............... MURDER
**JURISDICTION:** ............. STATE
**RACE:** ......................... WHITE
**SEX:** .......................... MALE
**AGE:** .......................... 17
**HEIGHT:** ...................... 6'-1"

**WEIGHT:** .................. 165
**HAIR:** ....................... SANDY BROWN
**EYES:** ....................... BROWN
**LAST KNOWN ADDRESS:** KILDARE IS. 231 BRADFORD ROAD, PELICA NC 27920

## CAUTION

Last seen wearing a tan "Bad Brains" t-shirt, striped board shorts, faded red hoodie, and sneaker Suspect may be traveling in a green 2003 Nissan Xtera, NC plates 1KE-F9C2. If you know the whereabouts of this person, please call 911 or contact the Kildare County Sheriff Department at 252-290-6688.

**T APPROACH - SUSPECT MAY BE ARMED AND DANGEROU**

The Kildare County Sheriff Department is offering a reward of $25,000 of gear for information leading to the apprehension of the suspect.

FOR

Remember that time everyone thought I died at sea?

That's called a summer bummer. —Kie

But our boy John B bounced back! —JJ

YOU CAN'T KILL A POGUE.

Pogue life got pretty wild.

But I'm getting ahead of myself.

98NH-D

Summers on the Outer Banks never used to be so complicated. The best part of Pogue life? Being neglected and ignored. We do what we want when we want.

Summer is all about catching rays and catching waves.

Lazy days spent fishing and drinking on the marsh.

Going wild and picking up the pieces afterward. —JJ

# MY CHILDHOOD

Back in the day, summers were also a time for some top-shelf quality hangouts with my dad. He taught me everything I know about the island and how to get by on it. How to fish. How to navigate the wilderness. The layout of the island and all the secrets it hides. And how to never let a Kook keep me down.

When I got older he sent me out fishing on the marsh alone. Maybe he knew one day I'd have to fend for myself. I'd be out on the water for hours, and then I'd hear a bell ringing from the Chateau. That was his way of calling me home.

Big John was a true quality dude. On nights I didn't want to go back home and deal with my dad, he always let me crash at the Chateau. —JJ

We would light up a campfire under the stars and throw together a big cookout with whatever fish I'd caught that day. And he taught me all about the constellations and how to navigate by the stars. How the North Star is the still point that everything else goes around. I really miss those times.

And he made the best banana pancakes. —Pope

Then the G-game started and everything went wild.

I can see my house from here.
—JJ

My dad was always into treasure hunting. He did two years at UNC Wilmington in archaeology and history, and he knew everything about all the wrecks off the coast of OBX. The Chateau was filled with books and maps he marked up on his searches.

When I was a kid I always begged him to let me join in, and when I was ten years old he finally taught me to scuba dive. I was so psyched to see what we could find under the waves.

The treacherous waters off the coast of the Outer Banks of North Carolina are known as the "**Graveyard of the Atlantic.**" Thousands of ships have sunk in the region since the sixteenth century, and countless mariners have perished.

HEAVY STUFF

I bet it's karma—all these colonizing sailors plundering the world's resources. All greed gets you is bad juju.
—Kiara

It was a combination of rough waves, unpredictable currents, atmospheric pressure, and shifting sandbars. It's just science, guys.
—Pope

I learned about people called "wreckers" who lured ships to their doom. They'd walk a horse along the shore at night with a lantern tied around its neck. The bobbing motion looked like a boat anchored safe in harbor, so the captains would follow . . . and crash right into the shoals. The wreckers would scavenge whatever they could.
—Sarah

While these wreckers sound like enterprising businessmen, you're all missing the most obvious explanation: the Bermuda Triangle. That's what it always leads back to.
—JJ

You blame everything on the Bermuda Triangle!
—Pope

# FAMOUS SHIPS THAT BIT IT OFF OBX

- Blackbeard's ship Queen Anne's Revenge
- Spanish galleon El Salvador
- Civil War ship USS Monitor
- Gunboat USS Huron
- Coastal steamer Pulaski
- Replica of the HMS Bounty

I bet there were generations of crazy lighthouse keepers.
—Kiara

We can't forget Scooter's grady-white which started the whole G-game!

Kraken got 'em.
—JJ

# THE ROYAL MERCHANT. THE BIG ONE.

The dream of generations of islanders. And no one had more dreams about the Royal Merchant than my dad. He put everything he had into his search. I guess I inherited his interest in hunting for it.

*You mean obsession. —Kiara*

Imagine this thing docked in Guffy's Marina

# MS Royal Merchant

MERCHANT, c.1813

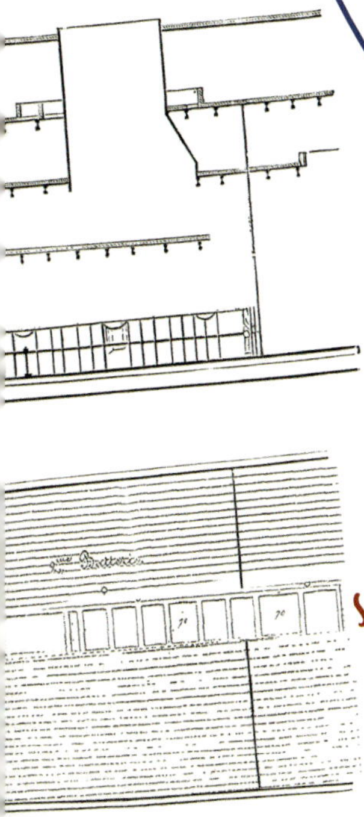


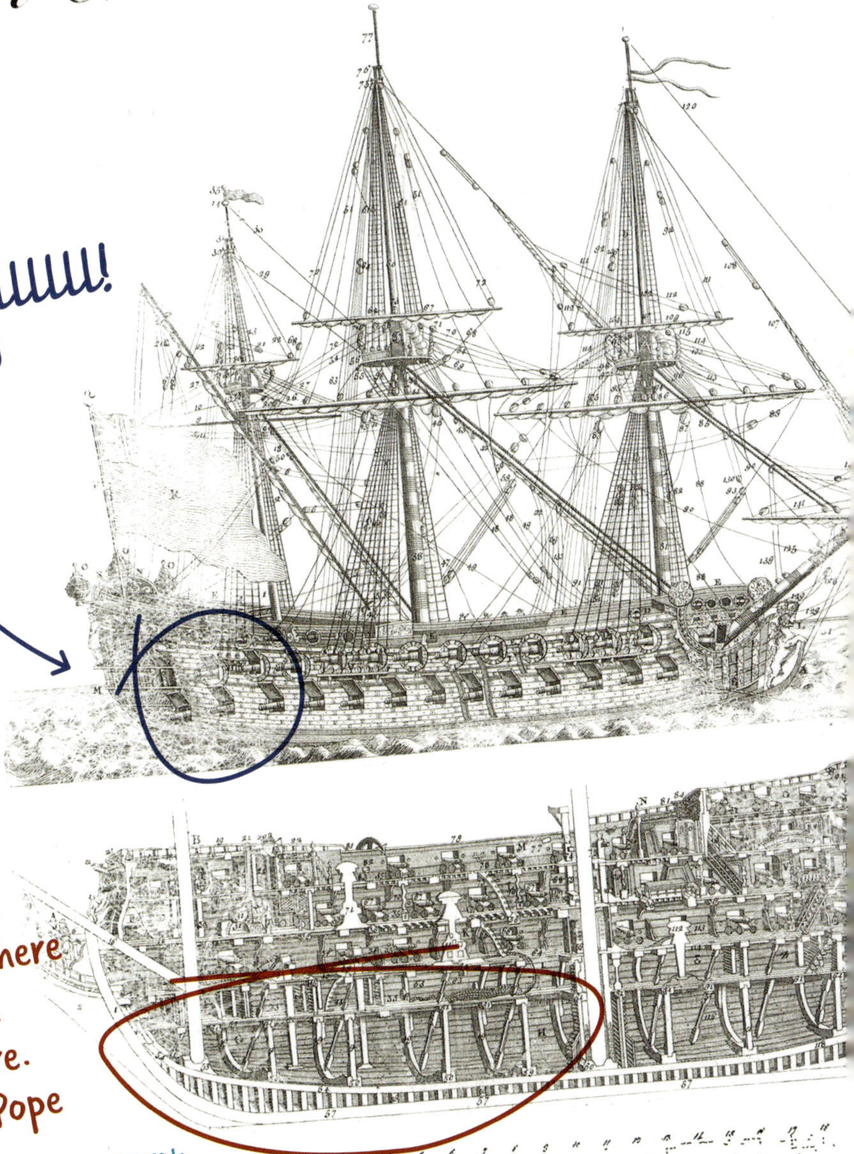

Cannonballlllll!
—JJ

The gold was somewhere in here.
—Pope

And the cross of Santo Domingo. —Sarah

2me Batterie.

2me Batterie.

Suite de la légende explicative.

# HMS *Royal Merchant*

Many shipwrecks have captured the imagination, but none has earned a place of legend like the *Royal Merchant*. Designed and launched from the Portsmouth Dockyard in 1822, she charted numerous voyages between the United Kingdom and its colonies. She had a reputation as a lucky ship, having survived an onboard fire as well as storms that sank lesser vessels. It was for this very reason in 1829 that the *Royal Merchant* was tasked with an important mission: delivering much needed supplies to the colonies and coming back with whatever spoils the *Merchant* could plunder. It would be her last voyage.

$400 million!!

The crew of the *Royal Merchant* was no stranger to rough seas, but its prowess would prove no match for the storm to come. One night, only miles from the Carolina coast, disaster struck from above. The great swells, lashing rain, and lightning that tore through the sky would soon become known as the Great Storm of 1829. Violent gales battered the ship, and she capsized and quickly sank beneath the waves. All forty-four crewmen aboard perished in the Graveyard of the Atlantic. Discovering the treasure of the *Royal Merchant* has become the dream of countless explorers. Yet so far, all searches for the gold have turned up empty-handed. Perhaps one day that will change. Perhaps an intrepid explorer will do what no one else has been able to. Perhaps that explorer . . . could be you!

Spoiler alert—except Denmark Tanny. —Pope

— Until the Pogues rolled up.

A SHIP of War, of the third Rate, With Rigging
Main Mast
Fore Mast
Mizzen Mast
Bow-sprit
Top-sail
Section of a SHIP of War, of ye First Rate, Shewing ye Inside.
Afore.
Fore Mast
Midships
Main Mast.
Abaft.
Mizzen Mast

# BIG JOHN'S SECRET NOTEBOOK

The British National Archives finally sent the logbooks I requested for the Rising Sun. She was a trading vessel returning from the West Indies that got diverted through the Graveyard of the Atlantic when the Great Storm of 1829 struck. The Rising Sun made it through safely while the Merchant sank. I always wondered why, and now I know—the logbooks' records of daily air pressure and wind force statistics support my theory that the Great Storm was weaker on the south end of the island. If the Merchant had only charted southward, she likely would have been spared. I referenced this with geological surveys to track how the shoreline shifted, and I predict the wreck of the Merchant lies around 34° 57' 30" N, 75° 55' 42" W. The high side of the continental shelf is around 800 to 1,000 feet deep. All this time, she's been closer to shore than anyone ever thought. The Merchant had the last laugh . . . until now.

I'm so close to zeroing in, I just need a little bit more cash to cover costs for one last push. A submersible drone and marine salvage gear ain't cheap. Ward balked when I brought it up. He got angry, called me greedy to ask for more money without any results yet. I do have results, but I'm keeping them close to the vest—I don't trust Ward Cameron as far as I can throw him. He's already profiting off my life's work. So I'll raise the cash myself. I've pawned what I could so far, but I don't want to ask John B to hawk anything of his yet. My son's already starting to lose faith in his old man. If only I could tell him how close I am to finding the gold. He'd finally understand my twenty years of searching wasn't a waste.

Manifest of the H.M.S. Royal Merchant 1829
MVP to Denmark Tanny
RIP to everyone else. —Kiara

One of my dad's big discoveries was the complete passenger manifest from the Royal Merchant. Other manifests didn't list the enslaved people aboard, but this one showed that Denmark Tanny worked as a cook. I wonder what it would have been like to be on the ship and what our roles would have been . . .

JOHN B:
CAPTAIN. Goes without saying, right?

JJ:
MASTER GUNNER. In charge of the cannons. Some powder, a fuse, and BAM!

*Are you sure putting JJ in charge of explosives is a good idea?*
*—Pope*

KIARA:
SHIP MUSICIAN.
We're gonna need a jam band to keep our spirits up for months at sea.

POPE:
NAVIGATOR.
So we don't get lost.

Or ship doctor for when JJ's cannonballs go haywire.
— Pope

SARAH: FIRST MATE.

To provide backup when I'm off being a heroic captain.

Why can't I be captain? Which one of us makes better decisions in dangerous times? —Sarah

. . . Fair point.

How about cocaptains?

# HOME SWEET HOME

The Chateau. The name may be the only fancy thing about it, but it's home. An old fish shack on the marsh that's been in my family for three generations. It's the perfect place to hang with my best buds all night and sleep in all morning.

Not as messy as it usually is. —Sarah

Gotta be prepared – never know when a girl might come over.

Is that right? —Sarah

Is this about to turn into a jam session? —Kie

The finest in outdoor dining.

Where JJ slept for like ten hours straight after eating the strongest special brownie known to man.

One of my greatest achievements.
—JJ

When this hammock's a-swinging, don't come a-ringing. —JJ

Empty fridge. Except for a six-pack of beer. Don't worry, JJ. —Sarah

Whew! —JJ

Empty shelves too. No wonder John B is always showing up at The Wreck for freebies. —Kie

# THE TWINKIE

Best set of wheels on the island. The Twinkie. A vintage Volkswagen Type 2. She's been through a lot, and she's never let me down. I bought the Twinkie when I was fifteen. I worked hard to afford her—extra early-morning shifts at Guffy's, odd jobs around town, anything I could do to scrounge up some extra dough. I could live in this thing.

**We basically have on road trips. —JJ**

The Twinkie's broken down like forty-five times, but I always patch her up and she keeps on rolling.

I named my van "the Twinkie" because it's shaped like . . . a Twinkie.

Definitely about to go get into some trouble. —JJ

When we're not getting into trouble on the streets of OBX, we're getting into it on the water.

**By land or by sea, we always find a way. —JJ**

Sometimes all you need for a good day is a boat and your best buds.

**Half a billion in gold would be nice too. —Pope**

The HMS Pogue used to belong to my dad. It's a Carolina Skiff he picked up forever ago. He taught me how to fish from it and how to navigate the channels. I basically grew up on this thing.

We've spent a lot of good days on the HMS Pogue chilling, taking siestas, drinking "juice boxes."

That means beer. —Kie

Remember when we hit a sandbar in the channel, discovered the sunken Grady-White, and started the G-game? Look what a day out on the water can lead to—besides a perfect tan.

Once we were out fishing and this giant tuna was circling our boat. We tried for hours to catch it. It became our "white whale." Kiara thought she could trap the tuna with a net. Pope thought he could outsmart it by causing vibrations in the water or something and luring the fish to us.

Everyone knows fish have otoliths to detect sound in the water.

—Pope

JJ tried to spear it. But the tuna got away in the end.

I'm still sore about that one. —JJ

Yeah, cuz you kept throwing a spear and missing. Get it?

—Pope

Maybe stick to fish anatomy instead of jokes.

—Sarah

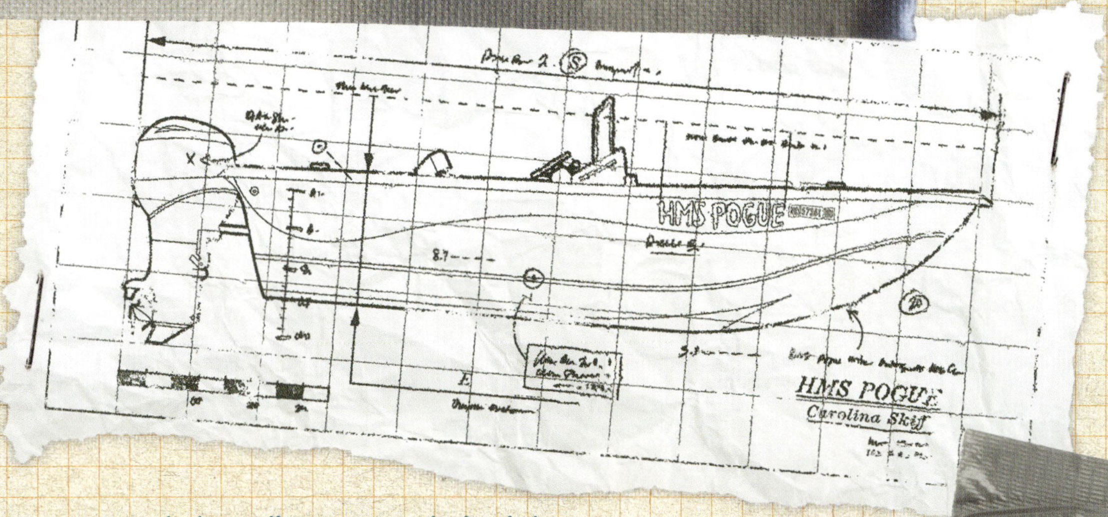


How about the time you tried to drag race against Topper out on the intercoastal? —Sarah

I wanted to show that frosted-tipped jerk that a boat's price tag doesn't mean anything if you don't know how to use it . . . But yeah, I lost the race by a mile. To be fair, though, Topper was racing a 2020 Malibu 24-MXZ. That thing's like $200,000 and loaded to the gills.

Still sank like any other boat when I pulled the plug . . . —Pope

# THE MY DRUTHERS

On an island with so many Kooks, the boats are gonna be pretty spendy. Like Ward's boat, the My Druthers. An eighty-two-foot Hatteras Skybridge. The finest in sporty luxury yachts. The kind of ship I dream about.

But the closest I ever got to a boat like that was working on it. Ward paid me to wash it clean, scrape off the barnacles, check that the electronics were in working order. One summer he asked me to first mate while he hosted a party aboard. Mostly I just mixed mai tais and made sure no one fell overboard. The Kooks barely noticed me, like I should be seen and not heard. Even Sarah. This was when she was still a Kook princess. Anyways, I always figured the boss's daughter was off-limits.

I noticed you. The cute first mate with the tousled hair and unbuttoned shirt. Then Topper noticed me looking and acted pouty the whole time.
—Sarah

Debating whether a "dreamboat" joke is necessary here . . .
—Pope

Then my job on the My Druthers ended after I got fired. But it was for the best. The My Druthers wasn't exactly the safest place for me to be that summer . . .

# MY GUIDE TO ESCAPING THE MY DRUTHERS

Ward went all psycho killer on me and I had to escape. Turns out an eighty-two-foot boat is a lot of boat to make it through.

1. First, panic that my girlfriend's dad is trying to kill me.

2. Struggle with Ward over gaff hook. Tumble over helm of boat.

3. Try to call in mayday to Coast Guard over VHF radio.

4. Dodge gaff hook slashes.

5. Thank the Big Kahuna for the cast on my arm. That thing saved my life!

6. Punch Ward in the face and run.

7. Fire speargun. Wish I had better aim.

8. Squeeze through bedroom hatch.

9. Wait for Jet Ski to lower. Why does it take so long??

10. Dodge spears. Be happy Ward doesn't have better aim.

11. Drop Jet Ski in water, kick the pedal, and ride like hell!

# GUFFY'S MARINA

Working as a dockhand at Guffy's Marina is pretty great. I wash down boats, polish machinery, top off the tanks, show clueless tourists how an anchor works. I like it, especially the tips. And I'm able to take the speedboats out for "test runs" and push that throttle to maximum speed. Gotta make sure everything's in tip-top shape!

I don't even mind cleaning up the boats after Kooks rent them out for parties. Look at everything they leave behind. Jackpot.

Finders keepers. That's unspoken maritime law. —JJ

Normally I'd say stealing is bad karma... but taking from Kooks might be deserved.
—Kiara

Cash

Cigars

Jar of caviar
(kinda gross)

Phone chargers

Monogrammed
lobster cracker

Lacrosse stick

Assorted flip-flops
that never match

Crystal champagne
holder I was gonna
hawk . . . till JJ
dropped and
broke it

Eighteen-inch pizza

So that's where that went! . . . Kidding! —Sarah

Slippery little sucker. —JJ

Please don't tell me you ate this. —Kie

I made him toss that one. —Pope

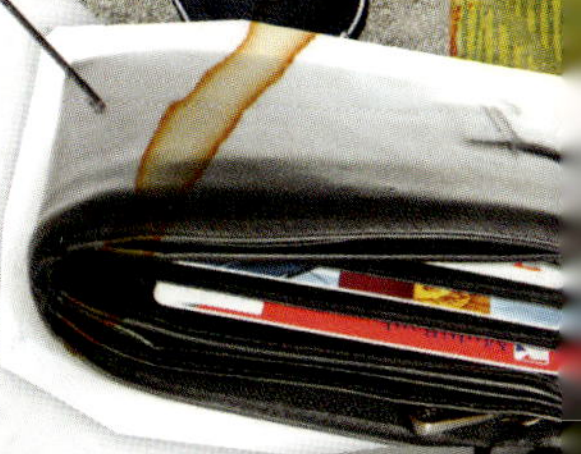

THE OUTER BANKS IS TWO TRIBES, ONE ISLAND. POGUES VS. KOOKS. SUMMERTIME = RUMBLE TIME.

Summer parties on the Outer Banks are like if Pogues and Kooks were stuffed into a keg together and shaken up: All it takes is one drunk idiot to make the whole thing explode.

I volunteer to be that drunk idiot. —JJ

# Ingredients for Any Good OBX Party

- Empty stretch of sand
- Keg or two or three
- Red Solo cups

- Bluetooth speaker for jams
- Sunscreen to offer to Tourons (really shows we care)

Tourons = Tourist Morons
—Pope

- Firewood and lighter fluid
- Lack of adult supervision

Pretty important
—Pope

- Best buds to have your back when Kooks try to drown you

Glad to be of assistance. —JJ

With the amount of fights that go down at parties, it's probably good to set a plan of attack.

## HOW TO TAKE DOWN A KOOK

First, let's be clear: It's always the Kooks who start it. I've got no choice but to defend. I'll deliver a brilliant insult. Then I'll try to de-escalate, but Kooks can be aggressive when provoked, so it's game on. Time for a shoving match.

Kiara will cause a distraction to throw the Kook off guard.

JJ will deliver a well-timed right hook, and we tag team a beatdown.

Pope will come up with a genius move to disorient the Kook, like pumping the keg and spraying him in the face with beer.

Sarah will be the lookout and give the signal when the police roll up, so we can book it out of there and not get caught.

Teamwork makes the dream work.
—Pope

# Department of Child Services

**KILDARE COUNTY COURT SYSTEM**

2325 North Main Street
Pelican, NC 27939
Phone: (252) 555.0174

**Cheryl Coleman**
*Chief Officer DCS*

# EVALUATION REPORT

In the matter of **Unemancipated Minor**
Division Section 17-24(a)
Industry/Area Unaccompanied Minor

To: **John B. Routledge**
At: 27 East River Road, Pelican NC - 27938

At the request of the Kildare County Department of Child Services, I have conducted an evaluation of John Booker Routledge in order to assist the department in coming to a decision in regards to his situation as an unemancipated minor living on his own. Despite his father being missing at sea for several months, Mr. Routledge has shown an unwillingness to face facts that his father may have abandoned him or may no longer still be alive. While all children experience the first stage of denial when it comes to the loss or abandonment of a parent, Mr. Routledge exhibits a steadfast belief that his father will be returning. Mr. Routledge claims his Uncle T is living at home as his legal guardian. While my efforts to locate and interview Uncle T have been unsuccessful, the house does in fact show signs of more than one individual residing there.

Mr. Routledge does not currently show signs of mental illness, psychological disorders, or aggression. By all accounts he is intelligent and well-adjusted, but prone to a stubbornness and denialism that could lead to volatile tendencies in the future.

Living the dream! —JJ

He's off building houses in Mississippi. Or Tennessee. Or maybe Idaho. Can't keep that guy pinned down.

Or three Pogues who crash on the reg. —Kiara

And never clean up after themselves!

Attestation:
I hereby certify that I have examined and compared this copy of the summons with the original and this is a true and correct copy of the original

Signature of officer serving the summons

South Carolina DCS
Child Support Enforcement
Cheryl Coleman

Sincerely,

Chief Officer DCS

SC-GOV24-24

SC DCS63 -17(a)

It's not like I'm getting into trouble all the time. But the Kildare County Department of Child Services doesn't see it that way. For some reason they don't think sixteen-year-olds should be living at home alone.

They missed all the concocting.
—Pope

And that he's prescription-grade distracted all the time. —Kie

And his refusal to button his shirts. That's a compulsive psychological disorder, right?
—Sarah

# REASONS I'M LATE FOR SCHOOL

Living at home with my best friends, no supervision, all the freedom in the world . . . It's enough to make anyone forget about high school. Which I kinda do ~~sometimes.~~

ALL THE TIME. —Pope

**TARDY SLIP**
(K)ILDARE COUNTY HIGH SCHOOL

Date *May 23, 2019*
(Admi)t *John B Routledge*
(to (C)lass) *History*
(Tim)e *9:25*
(Rea)son for Tardiness *Helping old lady cross the road.*
Principal

Real reason: Super hungover from playing wizard staff with JJ the night before. I won.

No way you won! . . . Actually I don't really remember. I taped up a pretty long wizard staff.
—JJ

**TARDY SLIP**
KILDARE COUNTY HIGH SCHOOL

Admit *John B Routledge* Date *April 9, 2019*
to (Class) *Math*
Time *9:55*
Reason for Tardiness *Alarm didn't go off.*
Principal

That's true . . . because my rooster escaped from the coop and ran off. Blame it on the rooster.

Maybe don't trust your punctuality to livestock?
—Pope

Da(te)
(Admit) *John B Routledge*
(to (Cl)ass) *English*
(Ti)me *9:38*
(R)eason for Tardiness *Claimed there was emergency at Guffy's Marina.*
(Prin)cipal

Real reason: It was an emergency. A Sunseeker 50M docked at the marina to refuel. That beauty is 162 feet long and goes for $60 mil! Guffy texted me about it. No way I was gonna miss driving over to stare and drool.

Boys and their boats.
—Sarah

KILDARE COUNTY HIGH

Date *March 16, 2019*

Admit *John B Routledge, Kiara Carrera, JJ Maybank, Pope Heywa*

to (Class) *History*

Time *2:20 pm*

Reason for Tardiness *Traffic jam all over island.*

Real reason: Okay, this day we just flat-out skipped. We had an all-night P4L hangout, passed out after a game of drunk horseshoes, and the next morning we saw the break was cresting with the cleanest of swells. We HAD to ride those waves. Mr. Sunn's history class could wait. So could algebra, and English, and biology . . .

Why take English anyway? I can already speak it.
—JJ

# OUR SURFER PROFILES

Finally my Photoshop skills come in useful.
—Pope

## John B Routledge

**FAVORITE MOVE:** Tube Ride — an ultimate classic.

**Description:** No matter what's out there on the water, Routledge never shies away from a challenge. Wipeouts can't keep this guy down. He brings energy, enthusiasm, and confidence to carve his way through the heaviest waves.

• SURFER PRO

Sarah

★ POGUES FOR LIFE

## Sarah Cameron

**FAVORITE MOVE:**
Floater — gliding weightless in style.

**Description:** Her father hired the best instructors to train her, but Sarah followed her own path instead. She enjoys independence on the water and always surprises with her moves. She's never happy to just go with the flow.

## JJ Maybank

**FAVORITE MOVE:**
Superman — a burst of aerial awesomeness.

**Description:** JJ enjoys being a show-off who goes for broke. He wants to get a reaction out of onlookers as much as he wants to make the drop. His fearless style always leaves something to remember.

• SURFER PROFILE •

JJ

UES FOR LIFE!

SURFER PROFILE

Pope

POGUES FOR LIFE

## Pope Heyward

**FAVORITE MOVE:** Roundhouse Cutback — steady control for maximum speed.

**Description:** Pope studied and analyzed pro surfers, concentrating on moves that deliver peak effectiveness. He thinks mental mastery is just as important as physical skill.

## Kiara Carrera

**FAVORITE MOVE:** Off-the-Lip — all drama.

**Description:** The first time Kiara hit the surf as a young girl, she could barely stand on her board. Then a pack of dolphins appeared alongside her and she took it as a sign to keep going. Now, before each run, she tries to feel at one with the waves.

# II

KILDARE SURF SHOP

JJ, you drive me crazy. Like, seriously. But there's no one I'd rather go crazy with. Getting into trouble, taking down Kooks, or plotting our international surf trip—I'll always be there with you, and I'll always be there when you need me. Kie

Hey, JJ, remember how I always thought you were John B's psycho friend? Well now you're mine, too, and that's pretty great. You always stick up for your friends and never take crap from anyone. You're a true role model. (Of Pogue friendship at least—let's not get too crazy here!)
—Sarah

JJ, you've been my best friend since the third grade. You're always up for an adventure, always down for a good time. Quick with a plan and full of bad ideas—but, like you say, stupid things have good outcomes all the time. And you're a better surfer than me—there, I said it.

John B

JJ, everyone thinks you're a bad influence on me . . . and yeah, they're probably right. But my life would be a lot more boring without you. You're the most loyal friend a Pogue could ask for, and we can always count on you to keep us on the edge of our seat—or push us off of it.

—Pope

# BEACH HAUL BLING

One time I convinced Big John to lend me his metal detector so I could scan the beach and turn up some bling to pawn. Hoped it could at least keep me stocked in Natty Light all summer.

My dad used it to scan the shores for shipwreck artifacts. —John B

# Beach Haul

- Coins in a language I can't read
- Aluminum fishing rod broken in half (Angry fisherman or monster fish?)
- Kildare Island souvenir key chain
- Brass necklace (I gave it to a summer honey named Shauna and told her it was made of gold. She found a great way to thank me that night.)
- Like a hundred pull tabs
- About a thousand bottle tops
- Probably two thousand bobby pins
- Set of dentures ← gross —Kie
- And my prized find: a vintage 1991 Red Hot Wheels Ferrari F40. Yeah, it's all corroded and shit and not worth much right now . . . but it's gonna be a collector's item someday.

It's not. —Kie

# MY GET-RICH-QUICK SCHEME$

If getting tons of gold and a gigantic golden cross doesn't work out, I've got some fallback ideas.

There are no natural oil reserves in North Carolina.
—Pope

1. Strike oil.

2. Start an aquaculture farm.

3. I've heard crypto is a thing.

4. Sue for medical malpractice—not sure for what, but I've got an uncle who says it's the best way to get one over on the Man.

5. Win the lottery.

6. Join a crime syndicate as a dirt bike getaway driver.

7. Marry rich. Sarah, you single?

You're a true romantic, J.J.
—Sarah

On second thought . . . I should probably stick to plan A. Gold, gold, and more gold.

# THINGS I WILL BUY AFTER WE GET THE GOLD

- International surf trip for my best buds
- A surfboard for every day of the week
- 1974 Yamaha YZ360 dirt bike — best of the best
- Marble statue of myself
- Upgraded version of Topper's Malibu — bigger, longer, better, faster *Why do guys always make it a boat-measuring contest? —Kiara*
- Pet monkey — a sign you're so rich you've gone mental
- Matching Pogue Jet Skis
- $24K blunt
- Private island
- Private security to punch Kooks when they get too close

The Cat's Ass. Best thing I've bought so far. Really ups the Chateau's property value while delivering the finest in luxury relaxation.

I thought "bar top" meant something else.

| | |
|---|---|
| Shell | Lucite Acrylic in Pearl Shadow |
| Water Capacity | 980 liters |
| Dimensions | 2,300mm x 2,400mm x 920mm |
| Control Panel | Gecko IN.K506 bar top control |
| Lighting | Underwater LED 6 Point Lighting |
| Jets | 49 stainless steel hydrotherapy jets in 5 varieties |
| Audio System | Full Bluetooth Audio with built in speakers and amplifier |

Big enough to fit five Pogues

Underwater EDM club

That shoot straight into your butt.

To pump that bass!

# A DAY AT SEA, JJ STYLE

Good things happen when you roll with the tides. Look at Denmark Tanny. Dude set out on the ocean and ended up a gazillionaire. I could even keep a journal like Denmark did.

And he only had to become the sole survivor of a devastating shipwreck!
—Kiara

11 a.m. Another early morning at sea. I dined on breakfast burritos and hearty ale.

Didn't exist.
—Pope

He's definitely gonna get scurvy.
—Sarah

It was smooth seas.

Then I noticed something swimming alongside in the depths below. Was it a dolphin? Ye old stingray? No, it was a smokin'-hot mermaid. Wavy hair, bangin' bod. Hotter than any figurehead I've ever seen on a ship's bow in all my days.

Definitely didn't exist.
—Pope

She wanted me to follow her. Who was I to deny her wishes? I went to the helm and yanked the

steering wheel to follow her toward whatever paradise island she would lead me to . . . But then I noticed something on my tail – a pirate ship! Skeevy-looking dudes aboard, up to no good. They were after my girl. So I commanded my crew to ready the cannonballs.

What's the old-timey version of an eye roll emoji
—Kie

oh now he has a crew at his command too? —Pope

I'm kinda into it.
—John B

Ready, aim, fire! BAM! One blast sent those pirates sky high and down to their watery graves. Then I jaunted off to a little beachside paradise with my ocean honey and we lived happily ever after. Also I found buried treasure. The End.

Guys, I think this is gonna be a bestseller. Want to hear about the sequel?

Nope! —Kie

I can't help it if my imagination runs a little wild. This is the Outer Banks. Think about where we've found ourselves: cemeteries, swamps, haunted houses. You gotta wonder: What else is lurking out there in the tall grass?

What's hiding under that log?

The answer is a gator. —John B

In ye old swamp, no one can hear you scream.

We gonna awaken an old curse and have to slay some Redfield zombies?

Hey, leave my ancestors alone. —John B

# LOCAL LEGENDS I MAY OR MAY NOT BELIEVE IN

This island is full of legends. I've overheard marina rats and salt lifers talk about 'em my whole life. One time my cousin Ricky treated a group of hikers who got all bit up by a wild animal, and the way he described those bloody wounds, no way it was your garden-variety animal bite.

- The Goat Man of Nags Head Woods
- Ghost Cat of the Cape Hatteras Lighthouse
- Blackbeard's ghost
- The White Doe
- Roanoke villagers – where'd they go?
- Ghost pirates of the Frying Pan Shoals
- And let's not forget the biggest monsters of all . . . C.H.U.D.

They're all true, look 'em up!

He had to bring up C.H.U.D.
—Kiara

Cannibalistic Humanoid Underground Dwellers. Just like the movie. I consider it more of a documentary. My friends don't get it, but they suffer from a lack of imagination — they just gotta crumble some herb and expand their minds.

The Newspaper for Today's Outer Banks • Breaking News 24/7 at obs

OUTER BANKS

**Gazette**

# Bizarre Gargoyle Fish Washes Up in Outer Banks

The Newspaper

OUTER BAN

**Gaz**

## Mystery Sea Creature Discovered on Kildare Island Beac

## Locals Claim Uniden... "Monster Fish" Drifted fr... Nuclear Facility Offshor

I was right about Old Lady Crain's house too. I knew she was hiding more than just her dead husband's head. Score one for JJ.

Everybody on the island knows the story. Crain killed her husband with an axe, chopped up the body, and got away with it.

**Gazette**

**Officers Called to Investigate Disturbing Sounds Reported at the Crain House**

**Gazette**

**Local OBX Man Disappears from Home Wife Investigated for Foul Play**

**Alma Crain No Longer Person of Interest in Husband's Disappearance**

**Locals Still Suspicious**

She nearly added me to her body count. But, like always, you can't kill a Pogue.

Legit scared shitless.
—Kie

And we did it — we found the gold!

Filthy FILTHY rich!
(for a moment anyway)
—John B

I love the Twinkie like she's my own flesh and blood. Come to Uncle JJ.

I love every spot of rust. I love that little hula dancer on the dash who shakes her hips and flirts with me. And what I really love are all the places that ol' J can hide his Mary J.

OBX

# My Favorite WEED HIDING SPOTS (just don't narc to Shoupe)

Tear in front seat upholstery

Passenger-side sun flap

It's crazy you haven't been busted yet. —Sarah

Behind air-conditioning panels

Not your brightest idea on a hot summer day. —John B

Bottom of console

Under floor mats

Tear in back seat upholstery

Inside Pope's pocket when he's not looking

Wait, what? —Pope

Secret compartment I'll never tell anyone about

Just like me, the Twinkie likes to make a statement. Gotta represent what we represent.

Got a sticker to hold together the windshield? —Kie

Waterproof decals for the win! —John B

Oceanfront paradise. —Kie

Private Island. —Pope

Get Gold. —John B

After everything we've been through, I think the Twinkie is due for some new slaps.

## New Twinkie Sticker Ideas:

- Won't Stop for Jets
- Goat Island Mud Run 2020
- This Vehicle Runs on Merchant Gold
- Denmark Tanny 4 President
- This Van Turns Kook Daughters into Pogues

True story.
—Sarah

# JJ'S STOLEN VEHICLE REPORT CARD

The Twinkie isn't the only set of wheels on the island we rode this summer. Sure, some we weren't legally allowed to use . . . but a little grand theft auto never hurt anyone.

## JORGE'S BICYCLE

Grade C

Good till John B yeeted over a chain and wiped out.

But Sarah brought me to Tannyhill to play nurse. Upgrade to a B. —John B

## SHOUPE'S SQUAD CAR

Grade B+

Good thing Shoupe sprung for the model with keyless ignition.

Even I'm impressed at that one. —Pope

## HEYWARD'S TRUCK

Grade F

Bum carburetor on the way to Charleston, then a crapped-out engine.

Not to mention almost running over me and John B! —Sarah

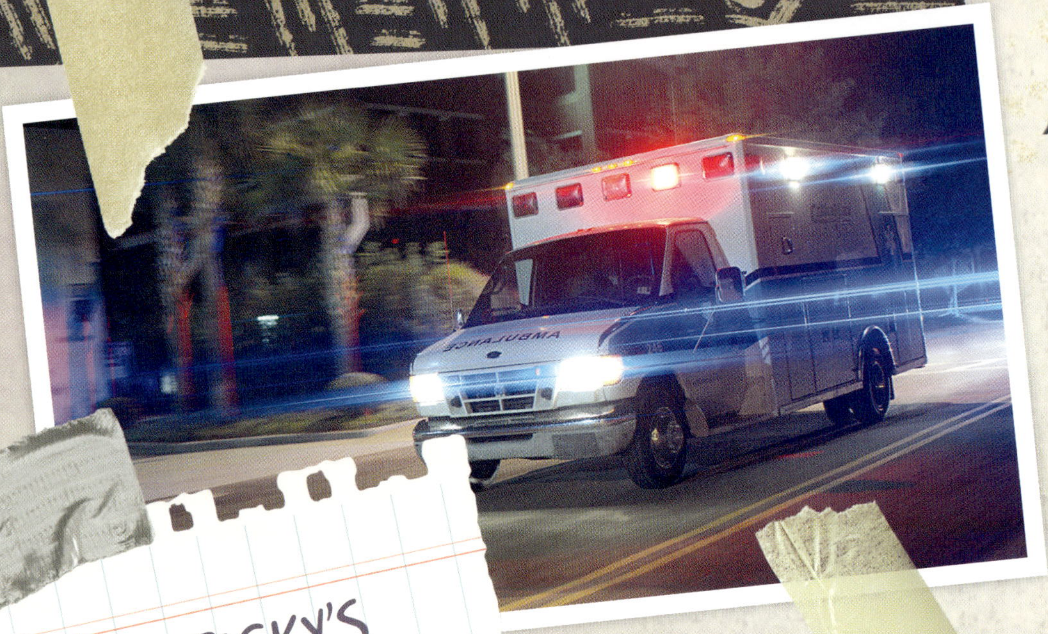

COUSIN RICKY'S AMBULANCE

Grade A+

My ridiculously genius idea to break John B out of prison.

*You mean just ridiculous. Grade F. —Kie*

## CHARLESTON PEDICAB

### Grade A

The site of our sweet, sweet family reunion. Now pedal, bitch! Work those quads!

## KIARA'S DAD'S TRUCK

### Grade B

The Twinkie gets by with a li'l help from her friends.

But I wigged out on a dose of adrenaline and totaled it. Sorry, Kie. I give myself an F. —Pope

I bought a dirt bike with my hard-earned green from last summer. I saved up from a little hustle John B and I had going on. Tourons flock to the island and wanna learn to surf. We were more than happy to provide an educational experience.

# *Summer* SURFING LESSONS!

With JJ and John B

"Safety first," that's my motto! . . . Psych. I never say that.

You guys are total liars. The "surfing lessons" were just a scheme to give your number to tourist girls and impress them. —Kie

It was so so obvious. —Pope

The scheme worked, though. Our phones lit up that summer with lovely ladies in need of some hands-on training. —John B

Uh . . . I'm retired now. —John B

Oh really? Is this still a future career path, John B? —Sarah

# JJ'S FOURTH of JULY

It's our patriotic duty
to have a rockin' time on the Fourth of July.

My cousin Ricky knew this chick, Hope, who knew this dude, Greg, who sells fireworks out the back of his Bronco. He trucks 'em in all the way from Tultepec. So Ricky got me the hookup on some Roman candles and we all chipped in. That night we went out to the marsh to set 'em off — those suckers shot up fifty feet high. Even higher than I was. Well, this Kook appears and starts squawking that we were gonna hit her house, and she calls the cops. Soon enough Shoupe rolls up and tell us to knock it off, so we hightailed it and drove to the Battery to act all pyro in peace. But Kelce and his Kook buddies were there doing the same thing. Kelce thinks he's some kind of military bro and starts a Roman candle shootout. It's like Battlefield: OBX down there. But for a guy who thinks he's a sharpshooter, Kelce's aim sucks and he hits a tree, which catches on fire, and then Peterkin's on the scene and you don't mess with her . . .

*Peterkin kicked everyone out so we went back to the marsh for round two and began all over again. —Kie*

# SUMMER JOBS I QUIT

I'm no company man, working for one place all my life. You can't tie me down. Gotta diversify that portfolio.

What JJ means is he keeps getting fired.
—Pope

## ISLAND CLUB BUSBOY

**Why I quit:** Kooks were talking smack about John B and Sarah. I wasn't gonna take that.

Nice try—you got canned for dumping a pitcher of water on Kelce and causing a scene.
—Pope

## KILDARE SURF SHOP RETAIL ASSOCIATE

**Why I quit:** I only worked there for a week to help myself to an employee discount.

Yeah, a <u>five-finger</u> discount, so they fired you. —Kiara

## PELICAN SPA TOWEL ATTENDANT

**Why I quit:** A very convincing guest requested I be her masseur. Sure, I wasn't licensed or anything, but who was I to deny a woman's wishes? Then she kept coming back and asking for me specifically, and I couldn't handle the clinginess.

Nope, I heard the spa owner found out and kicked you to the curb.
—Sarah

## E. REDD MATTRESS MART SALESMAN

**Why I quit:** That place was a total snooze-fest. I needed more excitement in my life.

The manager walked in and found you taking a nap.
—John B

Had to test the merch!

## MASONBORO BEACH LIFEGUARD

**Why I quit:** I'd rather be out on the waves than watching them from a tower.

So that's exactly what you did, and the boss canned you.
—Kie

# POGUES VS. THE PO-PO

Every cop on the island thinks of Pogues as future criminals. And yeah . . . they might be right. Shoupe issues us warnings all the time. But I like to think he appreciates it—everyone wants a fulfilling job, right?

LIST OF INCIDENTS:

- Going thirty over the speed limit racing the Twinkie through the Vanderhorst Estates
- Playing music too loud while partying out at the Creek
- Skateboarding in the police department parking lot
- Protesting with a loudspeaker in front of city hall

Had to make a statement at Occupy OBX. —Kie

When Kook kids get in trouble, all they need is their parents to glad-hand the sheriff and donate to the police fund.

Surprisingly itchy. —John B

→ Pogues aren't so lucky. We gotta stay one step ahead of the law, the Kooks, and everyone who wants to keep us down. And besides, prison stripes would harsh our style.

# REASONS I GOT IN TROUBLE AT SCHOOL

1. After some rich jackholes from the Kook Academy teepeed Kildare High, I snuck into the lion's den that night and cut my dirt bike across their football field. Tore up that grass real good—gotta defend the home turf by messing up theirs. My principal didn't see it that way, though.

*So unfair, you were delivering karmic retribution! —Kiara*

2. Sold candy outside the cafeteria during lunch . . . Okay, fine, the candy was weed gummies. But here's why it's not fair: I cut the gummies in half and sold 'em for my purchase price. My econ teacher should have been impressed instead of giving me detention.

Student's Name: JJ Maybank

Time: 10:45

Date of Incident: 2/16/2018

**DISCIPLINE NOTICE**

KILDARE COUNTY HIGH SCHOOL

CLASS - GRADE

The purpose of this report is to inform yo…

Nature of incident: *Failure to pay attention in class.*

Action taken: *Additional homework assigned.*

☐ Parents please sign and ret…

☐ Notice need not be returned

## 3. Failure to pay attention = me sleeping so hard I was left for dead.

*You were snoring way too loud to be dead.*
—Pope

I can't help it if the Constitution of the United States is boring. So many amendments to count, it's like counting sheep. So Mr. Sunn made me write an essay on "my favorite amendment and why." That was easy to look up: the Twenty-First Amendment to appeal Prohibition. Some true Pogue patriots must have come up with that one.

# MY POGUE CARE PACKAGE

## Wish List

IF I DO END UP IN THE CLINK, THIS IS WHAT I WANT MY FRIENDS TO SEND ME.

- Sunglasses
- Bar of soap
- Lighter
- Chocolate
- Flip-flops
- Cell phone
- Safety pin
- Gum
- Bottle of glycerin

As someone who was in prison and could have used an escape plan, I don't think any of this will be useful. —John B

Yeah, totally impractical. —Kie

I've got a plan, trust me. Always remember: stupid things have good outcomes all the time.

# MY ESCAPE PLAN TO BREAK OUT OF PRISON

If it's ever needed in the future. Fifty-fifty chance it will be.

1) Pop in some gum to go sweet talk the female nurse, start establishing a li'l flirtation. Minty fresh intro sets me apart from the rest.

This is pretty sus already. —Kiara

2) Offer her some chocolate. She sees how I'm willing to make a sacrifice to please her. She starts to develop sympathy for me. Everyone likes chocolate.

3) Trade cell phone with a corrupt guard for insider knowledge on the prison fire sprinkler system.

I think there are some corrupt cops up in Kildare County. —John B

4) Step into flip-flops and take a shower at the hottest water temp. Get that body temperature up. The flops aren't part of the plan, just cuz that shower floor is probably grody.

Literally the only smart part of this plan. —Kie

5) Rub the bar of soap on my face so I look pale as a ghost, then keel over and fake a burst appendix.

You're still going with this one? The success rate hasn't been great. —John B

Or as backup, eat the soap and force myself to hurl.

At least he's got a solid contingency plan. —Pope

6) Smear glycerin over my face to fake a sweat. Really sell the whole appendicitis thing. When the nurse sees me, she remembers the chocolate and the minty flirting. She's all sympathy. Calls for an ambulance right away, doesn't even bother to take vitals.

7) Hold the lighter up to the ceiling fire sprinklers. Sprinkle city. It causes pandemonium. Guards are so busy they don't even ride along in the back of the ambulance. They just handcuff me to the stretcher.

8) Use the safety pin I've hidden in my prison jumpsuit to undo my handcuffs. I watched a YouTube video, I've got it down.

Sure, that's of course how it works. —Sarah

Sneak out the ambulance door before they even know I'm gone.

9) Stroll on out of there to freedom and throw on shades so I look chill AF. This plan is foolproof!

# PEOPLE WHO TRIED TO KILL US

Ward Cameron

Killer Kooks. The whole Cameron family is psycho (no offense, Sarah). Where's DCS when you need them?

Tried to gaff-hook me on the My Druthers. Paid off an inmate to try to strangle me. Murdered my father over the gold.
—John B

Locked me up, kidnapped me, faked his own death, manipulated me, and basically lied to me my entire life. —Sarah

Rafe Cameron

Shot at me on the tarmac. Shot at me in the Nassau cane fields. Lit the bell tower on fire with me inside. —John B

Lit the bell tower on fire with me inside too. Actually shot me in the Nassau cane fields. Tried to drown me by the docks. —Sarah

Encouraged Topper to beat me senseless. Tried to shoot me in the swamp. Fed Renfield to the gators. —Pope

Tried to drown me in a storm drain. —Kiara

Almost shot me up in the treetop outside the Chateau.

Seriously, WHAT is with Rafe? —Kie

Carla Limbrey

This nutjob is practically genteel.

She hides behind her manners and her bribes and pays people to do her dirty work. —Pope

Renfield

Threatened us with sharpshooter archers and took Pope's family key. —John B

Tried to kidnap me. Punched me in the kidneys. Beat up my dad. —Pope

At least dude is gator food.

Square Grouper Boys

Shot at us on the HMS Pogue to get my Dad's compass. Wrecked his office and took his merchant research. —John B

Those bros are shark bait now.

Fun fact: Maritime drug smugglers were called "square grouper boys" because they trafficked shipments by dropping square-shaped bales of weed into waterways. —Pope

Batshit old lady with a shotgun I could barely even see! —John B

She came after me and Kie with a fire poker! —Sarah

Murderous Prison Inmates

Tried to strangle me, but I kick-flipped my way to safety. Remind me not to end up in prison again.

I have no idea what he looks like! He could be anyone, he could be out there somewhere . . .
—John B

Barry the Drug Dealer

Slimeball who took the gold nugget at gunpoint. But I got my revenge—dude is 25K lighter now.

# WHAT WE FOUGHT BACK WITH

## FISTS
The OG weapon

## COMPASS
Clues from the great beyond. My father's lucky compass. —John B

## FAKE KEY
Fake Island Room key we gave to Limbrey. —Pope

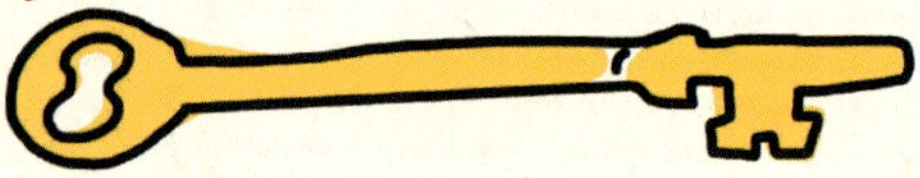

## CAMCORDER
To film Ward meeting with Gavin the pilot. —Kie

## THE TWINKIE

Blocker of planes

## SPYGLASS

Denmark's spyglass —Pope

With bonus secret message.

"You've come this far, do not falter. The cross is on the Freedman's altar." —Pope

## POPE'S BRAIN

The architecture of two-hundred-year-old churches can hide giant crosses within the beams.

Mosquitoes are attracted to water.

Gold makes planes heavy.

# KIARA

Kiara, you're funny, passionate, resourceful, a rebel, and the coolest person I know. In fact, you're so cool I always thought you'd finally see the light and go run with another crew. But that's not how you roll. No matter what happens I know we've got each other's backs, and I can't ask for more than that, right?

→ Pope

Kie, we were best friends in the 9th grade, then worst enemies in the 10th, and I really missed you. Now I can't wait to make up for lost time! You march to the beat of your own drum, and it makes me want to do the same. And, of course, we both know the guys would be totally lost without you. —Sarah ♡

Kiara, I've still never figured out what a girl like you is doing slumming it with guys like us. But I sure am glad you are. You're a Pogue through and through, the glue that keeps us all together. And if there is a karmic balance like you say, you're definitely keeping us on the good side. Diver down, Kie.

—John B

Yo, Kie! You're the best super-hot-rich socialist hippie chick I know (actually, you're the only one I know). I'm happy you're ditching all your parents' expectations to hang with us. Your Pogue family is where it's at! Here's to more good vibes and good times with you and me.

— JJ

I'm all about catching those OBX summer vibes . . . but I figure why not send some good vibes back out into the universe? Tip the scales and try to make this island a better place? There's a cosmic balance and I gotta make up for all the negative Kook energy.

# TURTLE HABITAT RESTORATION!

A cleanup campaign to help our little friends. Sunday, June 6. Meet at the pier information kiosk at 6 a.m.!

I remember this! We actually got a bunch of people out to help us. Everyone loves a cute baby turtle. —Sarah

Except my so-called friends. They didn't show!

You expected us to roll out of bed at that hour?? —John B

Dawn patrol and JJ Maybank don't mix. —JJ

SAVE OUR STREAMS!
OCCUPY OBX!
POWER TO THE PEOPLE!
MEET IN FRONT OF
LET OUR VOICES

I've got some ideas for worthy campaigns that islanders can donate to . . .
—JJ

- JOHN B HAIRCUT FUNDRAISING WALK-A-THON
(my boy's lookin' a little shaggy)

- DRINKING FOR A CAUSE
(the cause is me getting drunk)

JJ, I think we have different definitions of "worthy."

- XCALAK EXPEDITION GRANT
(support my cultural immersion)

- JJ BAIL FUND
(my teachers are always telling me I gotta plan for the future)

# Rock the OBX

A couple summers ago I volunteered to perform a song at the big Rock the OBX Festival. My parents were thrilled, they thought I'd do some sweet campfire song and make new Kook friends . . . But I got up onstage with my ukulele and began singing "Get Up Stand Up" by Bob Marley and the Wailers— and I changed the words a little . . .

"GET UP STAND UP,
STAND UP FOR YOUR RIGHTS!
GET UP STAND UP,
BRING THE KOOKS A FIGHT!"

The whole thing was about fighting Kook oppression. The crowd was NOT into it. My mom was so pissed, she looked like she was gonna charge onstage and chuck my uke into the sea.

Rose said you were a bad influence and didn't want you coming to Tannyhill anymore. I was never prouder to have you as a friend. —Sarah

I got booed offstage, which sucks because I had an entire Marley set list all about Kook greed. One day I'll do a covers album.

# MY TWINKIE DJ PLAYLIST

## Every summer joyride needs a soundtrack

1) "Blitzkrieg Bop" — Ramones
2) "The Harder They Come"—Jimmy Cliff
3) "Hit the Road Jack"—Ray Charles
4) "Novacane"—Frank Ocean
5) "What's Going On"—Marvin Gaye
6) "Sunday Morning"—No Doubt
7) "Anarchy in the U.K."—Sex Pistols
8) "Equal Rights"—Peter Tosh
9) "All My Best Friends Are Metalheads"—Less Than Jake
10) "Simmer Down"—Bob Marley & the Wailers
11) "Rudy, a Message to You"—Dandy Livingstone
12) "I'll Stand By You"—Pretenders
13) "Wrong Way"—Sublime
14) "Ain't No Mountain High Enough"—Marvin Gaye & Tammi Terrell

OBX

Pogues

Don't mess with Kiara's playlist order.
It drives her crazy! —John B

I can't help it if I have good taste in music.

Nobody wants a dictator DJ. That's why the rest of us made a playlist too. C'mon, Kie, you say everyone should have equal rights — that includes control of the dial, right? —JJ

1) "Left Hand Free"—Alt-J
2) "Left with a Gun"—Skinshape
3) "Texas Sun"—Khruangbin & Leon Bridges
4) "Paper Planes"—M.I.A.
5) "Crashed My Bike"—Sun Room
6) "Dare"—Gorillaz
7) "Bad Kids"—Black Lips
8) "Hot Stuff"—Kygo & Donna Summer
9) "Left Me Like Summer"—Daily J
10) "Ain't No Rest for the Wicked" —Cage the Elephant

THERE WAS A TIME IN NINTH GRADE I GOT KINDA INTO WITCHCRAFT. NO ONE ELSE TOOK IT SERIOUSLY EXCEPT SARAH. AT SLEEPOVERS WE READ OUR TAROT CARDS AND TRIED TO CAST SPELLS TO MAKE BOYS LIKE US.

Which boys? —John B

We'll never tell. —Sarah

Remember we made a voodoo doll of that girl who was a total bitch to us in algebra class?! —Sarah

We even snuck into the cemetery to have a séance for my pet hermit crab. RIP Kingston. Hope you're enjoying that big shell in the sky.

So, Kie, you believe in séances for dead hermit crabs but you don't believe in C.H.U.D.?? —JJ

This island does have a creep factor — and we just keep finding ourselves in the middle of it. There's some bad juju in the air.

Blame Kooks. Always blame Kooks. —Pope

With a lighthouse that tall, you think there'd be fewer shipwrecks. —Sarah

Total workplace hazard up there. —John B

Gotta be some ghosts chilling around there.—JJ

Angel Oak must look super haunted at night.

# MY POGUE ASTROLOGICAL READINGS

**SAGITTARIUS:**
Sagittarians are idealistic with a good sense of humor. They like freedom and to keep life exciting by seeking new experiences. They have a wide circle of friends and enjoy being the center of attention. They're drawn to partners who can keep up with them. They dislike clingy people and being constrained in restrictive relationships.

*Kie, it's like you're peering into my soul! —Sarah*

**LEO:** Leos are loyal and optimistic with a magnetic personality. Brave leaders. Self-assured and restless. They sometimes think the world revolves around them, and they can be very stubborn!

No way, I am NOT stubborn.

—John B

**AQUARIUS:** Aquarians are revolutionary thinkers with strong convictions who want to change the world. They're nonconformists and rebels at heart. They're able to see the best qualities of their friends, even when other people don't. But Aquarians can be so focused on shaking things up that they neglect their family, friends, and romantic partners.

*Sounds like Kie. —John B*

**VIRGO:** Virgos are logical, practical, precise, systematic, and resourceful. They're perfectionists who want to help their friends. They can be so worried about making errors that they forget to have fun.

*Pope? Forget to have fun? Never. —JJ*

*I don't believe in this stuff because it's not logical . . . but that is pretty spot on. —Pope*

**ARIES:** Aries are fierce, courageous, and quick to action. Permanent cheerleaders for their friends. They will fight for their friends harder than they fight for themselves. They're also risk-takers who like to party hard. But beware, they can get caught in a cycle of negativity when things go wrong in their lives.

I always thought astronomy was a little woo-woo, but that's not too far out. —JJ

You mean astrology. —Pope

What's the difference? —JJ

# THE WRECK RESTAURANT

*Fish and Crab House*

WHEN I'M NOT DISAPPOINTING MY PARENTS WITH MY LIFE CHOICES, I WORK AT THEIR RESTAURANT, THE WRECK. I BASICALLY GREW UP THERE, AND I FILL IN FOR EVERY JOB THERE IS: WAITRESS, HOSTESS, LINE COOK, DISHWASHER, JANITOR, AND PROFESSIONAL TASTE-TESTER.

Need a new coworker? —JJ

My mom grew up rich on Figure 8, but then she met my dad and dropped out of college to start the restaurant with him. The place is popular with everyone — Pogues, Kooks, tourists — they all want what The Wreck serves up.

The best part of working there is sneaking my friends in after closing and dipping into the leftovers.

We think that's the best part too.
—Pope

Beer-Battered Fish is clearly the winner. —JJ

Crispy Fish Tacos by a mile. —John B

Beer-Battered Fish = fish and beer. Two major food groups in one. —JJ

Crispy Fish Tacos have it all. Creamy and crispy. Salty and spicy. —John B

You know what they don't have? Beer. —JJ

Call it a draw and order both? —John B

# THE WRECK Fish and Crab House RESTAURANT

## STARTERS

- Hush Puppies . . . $6.00
- Hot Crab Dip . . . $12.00
- Blue Crab Nachos . . . $15. 00

Pogue-approved —JJ

## SOUP & SALAD

- Crab Bisque . . . $7.00
- Corn Chowder . . . $7.00
- House Salad . . . $6.00

## DESSERTS

- Key Lime Pie . . . $8.00
- Sweet Potato Pie . . . $8.00

## MAINS

- Beer-Battered Fish . . . $13
- Mahi-Mahi Burger . . . $12.
- Crab Cake Sandwich . . . $1
- Crispy Fish Tacos . . . $ 11.00
- Fried Oyster Po'boy . . . $11.0
- Spicy Pimento Shrimp and Grits . . . $11.00

## SIDES

- Hoppin' John . . . $6.00
- Fried Green Tomatoes . . . $5.00
- Baked Potato . . . $5.00
- Old Bay Fries . . . $5.00

"Kie" lime pie
(sorry, I had to). —Sarah

Remember we rolled in one wild Saturday night and ate every single leftover in the kitchen? We might have had the munchies.

We could barely move afterward. Worth it. —Pope

One day we were short-staffed during the lunch rush, so I went to help in the kitchen . . . but I accidentally dumped a bowl of pimento cheese into a pot of shrimp and grits. I didn't want to piss off my dad, so I kept quiet . . . but diners started complimenting the "spicy shrimp and grits." I finally came clean — and instead of getting mad, my dad put it on the menu. It's been a bestseller ever since.

## KIARA'S SPICY SHRIMP AND GRITS

4½ cups water
1 cup stone-ground grits
2 dried bay leaves
1 cup pimento cheese
4 teaspoons Tabasco or hot sauce of choice
1 tablespoon butter
Salt and freshly ground pepper
4 ounces thick bacon, cut into ½-inch strips
1 pound peeled shrimp
2 teaspoons lime juice
½ cup chopped parsley
1 tablespoon olive oil

Everyone knows I don't like following directions. Someone want to make this for me? —JJ

You doing the dishes afterward?

**Step 1**

Bring water to a boil in a medium saucepan and add grits and bay leaves. Bring back to a boil, then reduce heat to medium-low. Cover and cook, whisking often and scraping the bottom of the pan so the grits don't get stuck. Cook until grits are creamy and thick, around 30 to 40 minutes. Add more water if necessary. If grits are too watery, cook for a few minutes longer. Once grits are ready, increase heat to medium. Remove bay leaves and discard. Stir in cheese, Tabasco, and butter until cheese is melted and mixture is smooth. Season with salt and pepper to taste. Remove from heat and cover. Note: If using quick-cooking or instant grits instead, cook according to package directions, then stir in cheese and seasonings.

**Step 2**

Heat oil in a skillet over medium-high heat. Cook bacon until crispy, about 5 minutes. Place on paper towels to drain.

**Step 3**

Increase heat to high and cook shrimp in skillet in batches until cooked through, about 1 minute per side. Transfer shrimp to a bowl and add lime juice, parsley, bacon, a dash more hot sauce, and some salt and pepper. Mix everything to combine.

**Step 4**

Ladle grits into bowls and top with shrimp mixture.

I'm sure the rich people of Kildare Island have been hosting fancy events like Midsummers before the Island Inn Resort was even built. Just swap the Bentleys and DJ for horse-drawn carriages and a violin quartet. Different era, same Kooks.

*The honor of your presence*
*is requested to attend the*
*coronation of*
*Ward Cameron*
*during the annual*
*Midsummer Gala*
*to be held at the*
*Island Inn Resort*
*Kildare Island*
*Friday, July 19th*
*Two thousand and nineteen*
*at seven o'clock*
*by the*
*Joint Committee of the*
*Knights of the Rhododendron*

Silly Kook events like the Midsummer Gala are soooooo important to my parents.

You should see Ward and his precious Knights of the Rhododendron!
—Sarah

They think my future is gonna be ruined if I don't go.

## Ridiculous Things I Saw at the Midsummer Gala

- ICE SCULPTURES IN THE MIDDLE OF SUMMER
- A MAN HAVING AN ALLERGY ATTACK OVER HIS WIFE'S FLOWER TIARA
- SOUP SHOOTER HORS D'OEUVRES —WHO WANTS TO THROW BACK A SHOT OF HOT SOUP? AND ALL THAT SINGLE-USE PLASTIC IS JUST GONNA END UP IN THE OCEAN!
- LIKE TWELVE DIFFERENT SHADES OF PINK PASTEL
- ROSE'S SPIKY GOLD CROWN GETTING SNAGGED ON DRAPERY— THAT ONE WAS ACTUALLY PRETTY GOOD.
- FIVE DIFFERENT BOW TIES WITH PATTERNS OF HUNTING DOGS
- A TAXIDERMY PHEASANT
- WHITE PEOPLE DANCING BADLY

A FEW SUMMERS AGO MY MOM LEFT AN ISLAND CLUB EVENTS SCHEDULE ON MY BED. SHE SERIOUSLY THOUGHT IT WOULD MAKE ME WANT TO JOIN IN! THESE KOOK EVENTS NEED NEW NAMES THAT TELL THE TRUTH OF WHAT THEY ARE.

Rose dragged me to that one. It was total patriarchal oppression. —Sarah

I'll tell you what they actually are—Kooks trying to keep Pogues in their place. —JJ

Island Inn®

EVENT SCHEDULE

WEDNESDAY, JULY 8

~~Local Business Owners Luncheon~~

Capitalist Greed Society

FRIDAY, JULY 10

~~Debutante Ball Planning Committee Kickoff~~

Patriarchal Oppression Committee Kickoff

TUESDAY, JULY 14

~~Ballroom Dancing Lessons~~

Kooks Still Can't Dance Workshop

SUNDAY, JULY 19

~~Private Youth Golf Competition~~

Kook Indoctrination Event

WEDNESDAY, JULY 22

~~Flower Arranging Seminar~~

Rich People with Too Much Time on Their Hands Seminar

I can't believe this is how the other half lives.
—Pope

October 3rd—First week of Kook Academy and it SUCKS, just like I knew it would. I don't have anything in common with anyone, and all the stuck-up Kooks roll their eyes at me and act like I don't exist. In the cafeteria, a dude with a popped collar saw that I brought food from The Wreck for lunch and said loudly for everyone to hear: "Guess the leftovers do go straight in the trash." Everyone laughed, and I was about to get up and stuff a crab cake all over his stupid, smug face... But then Sarah Cameron sat down next to me. She started talking like we were already in the middle of a conversation. Like we had been friends for years. She made sure everyone saw it too. I thought I was being pranked. She's the Kook Queen and she was actually being NICE TO ME? Then Sarah asked if I wanted to go down to the beach that weekend to save baby sea turtles. I couldn't believe it. There had to be some kind of catch... but there wasn't.

I could just tell there was a good person beneath the scowl! —Sarah

Tell me which Kook jerk insulted you? We'll give him more than a crab cake to the face. —John B

November 2nd—Went to Sarah's for a sleepover last night. Tannyhill is actually pretty cool. Yeah, Kooks are still basically the devil, but maybe hell isn't always the worst place to visit. First, we swiped beers from Ward's fridge and talked shit about everyone at school. Then we ordered pizza and watched clips from our favorite movies on her laptop until the battery ran out. Then we stayed up till 2 a.m. telling each other our deepest, darkest secrets. It was literally the best time ever. I never thought I'd become good friends with someone like Sarah, but I was wrong. Maybe this whole Kooks vs Pogues war doesn't always have to stay that way . . .

Nice try Kiara! —JJ

Ah, the innocence of youth.
—Pope

So glad we became friends again, Kie. You're the best.
—Sarah

# PIRATE PROFILES

SUMMERS ON OBX WOULD MEAN NOTHING WITHOUT MY FRIENDS. THERE'S NO ONE I'D RATHER GET WASHED UP ON A DESERT ISLAND WITH.

*Let's hope THAT doesn't happen.*
*—Sarah*

*I think we could handle it. We'll just start our own pirate crew.*

**KIARA'S PIRATE SKILLS:**

- Swordfights with scallywags
- Fellow pirate recruitment
- Cooking meals when the only food for miles are coconuts
- Defusing tension with a relaxing tune on the fiddle

**JJ'S PIRATE SKILLS:**

- Scaring children with hook
- Using hook to slice through ship sails and slide down during skirmishes
- Reflecting hook in sunlight as signal beacon
- Macking on mermaids and sirens
- Brewing up rum in barrels

**POPE'S PIRATE SKILLS:**

- Navigating using maps and instruments
- Looking out for enemy pirates in pursuit
- Setting booby traps
- Preserving seafood in accordance to Heyward's Seafood Safety Protocols

**JOHN B'S PIRATE SKILLS:**

- Keeping ship on course
- Painting skull and bones on flags
- Locating deserted island spots to bury treasure
- Evading maritime law in multiple countries

**SARAH'S PIRATE SKILLS:**

- Parrot tamer
- Sewing up sails that JJ rips with hook
- Shopping for supplies at ports of call
- Charming Kook vacationers to donate provisions

# POPE

Yo, Pope, you're a super-weird dude. But you're our super-weird dude. You're a best bud till the end, and you've got the brightest future of us all—so don't let me screw it up for you! —JJ

Pope, you're the smartest dude I know. The brains of this whole operation and the voice of reason I never listen to—but maybe I should, because you're usually right. I don't always know what to make of you, but I know the Pogues have it made because you're one of us.

—John B

Pope, you're one of a kind and I don't know what I'd do without you. You can be Party Pope, Boring Pope, Polite Pope, Brainy Pope . . . but no matter what Pope you're gonna be on a given day, I'm just happy to always have you in my life.

—Kie

Pope! The island's best mathlete, future coroner, and all-around great guy. Without you the other guys wouldn't stand a chance. Never change, Pope. Just don't forget about us when you get your ticket off the island! —Sarah

Remember when I learned I'm related to Denmark Tanny? I don't think it gets much wilder than that.

I think that makes you the rightful Lord of Tannyhill. —John B

Denmark survived the Merchant wreck, dragged the gold to shore, and used it to build Tannyhill. Then he paid for the freedom of all the slaves on the island and built them a church.

Don't let the fancy threads fool you, dude's an OG Pogue. —JJ

Total Pogue in Kook's clothing. —Kie

Denmark even kept his own scrapbook while he worked aboard the Merchant. Same Pogue wavelength. I like to think he'd be stoked that his descendant is gonna reclaim what was rightfully his.

*If I am to be confined to working the kitchen of the Merchant, I shall endeavor to keep my spirits heightened. While my brethren below deck carouse into the night with purloined ale and porter, I find it of better use to be of sound mind and to rise early with a clear head. I find it prudent to exercise great judgment of mind and body, and to care for the vitality and health the good Lord has decided fit to deem me with. I know there is a world and a providence awaiting me beyond the confines of this ship.*

Denmark was also an artist. This guy could do it all!

Denmark got the Cross of Santo Domingo off the sinking Merchant. Dude was clearly an overachiever. I feel like such a slacker — I couldn't even get a merit scholarship!

Total BCE. Big Cross Energy. —JJ

The Cross of Santo Domingo was a gift from New Spain to the Spanish king, widely considered to be the most extravagant tribute ever from the provinces. It was lost off the coast of Bermuda in 1829.

I've never been a religious man, but the sight of this beaut just might make me a believer. —JJ

Some have said the Cross of Santo Domingo is cursed, for His holy symbol has been sullied with gold and jewels demonstrating man's worldly greed. Others say the cross holds proof of His divine power. There is a compartment locked within it and inside lies a shroud. Merely a simple length of linen cloth, yet there are those who claim it works miracles. To simply touch it will heal the sick of their maladies in an instant. Witnesses testify even those near death can be cured. I don't profess to know the truth, but tragedy brought this cross to us and I fear more tragedies may still yet unfold.

No wonder sailors thought this thing was cursed. Captain Limbrey stole it from another ship and left the men to die. This thing DEFINITELY has bad juju. —Kie

I dreamt of swiftly taking action to halt the atrocity and rescue the men of the San Jose. But any who question Captain Limbrey are met with swift punishment. Once the cross was steadily upon the Merchant, he looked upon it with such zeal nothing could release him from his trance. Neither flame nor cries of anguish could shake him.

The Outer Banks has tribal dynamics just like any ecosystem. And Pogues and Kooks can be classified just like any other species.

Nerd alert!
—JJ

# ADVANCED PLACEMENT OBX STUDIES

## KOOKS

- Superiority complex
- Punchable face
- Polo shirt
- Golf club
- General lameness
- Braided belt
- Salmon shorts
- Expensive boat shoes

## POGUES

- Salty hair
- A face that could get away with anything
- Bandana
- Bracelets
- Old T-shirt
- General awesomeness
- Board shorts
- Pair of beat-up Converse

You mean vintage.
—Kiara

Hope both are wearing sunscreen. UV protection transcends tribes!
—Sarah

Pogues = bottom of the food chain but looking fly as hell. —John B

# WILD ANIMALS THAT ATTACKED US

Whoever said "Living in paradise is no vacation" sure was right.

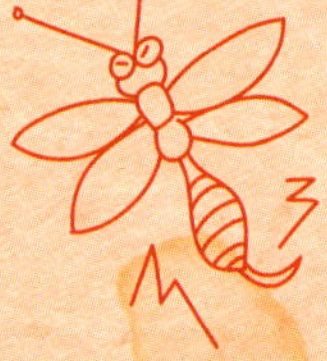

## WASPS

Fun fact I discovered this summer—I'm allergic to wasps!

Thank the Big Kahuna for Cousin Ricky's supermax dose of adrenaline!
—John B

## SNAKES

Kiara braved venomous water moccasins to crawl into the Redfield family crypt.

The things I do for my friends. Why did it have to be snakes? —Kie

## JELLYFISH

Sarah got stung by jellyfish when we stranded her and Kie in the marsh. Fun fact: peeing on a jellyfish sting doesn't actually help . . .

Luckily JJ left me with another way to help the pain . . .
—Sarah

Always looking out for my friends. —JJ

# ALLIGATOR

**John B got attacked by a gator!**

That thing had like a thousand teeth. —John B

Eighty, in fact.

Quick, call Kildare Animal Control!

At least we haven't encountered any great white sharks, tiger sharks, and bull sharks . . . yet.

Don't tempt fate, Pope! —Sarah

Pretty sure I can take down a shark. —JJ

# WILD PLACES WE ALMOST DIED AT

Maybe JJ is right, and we should chuck it all and head to Xcalak. Probably safer than it is here.

I've been trying to tell you guys. —JJ

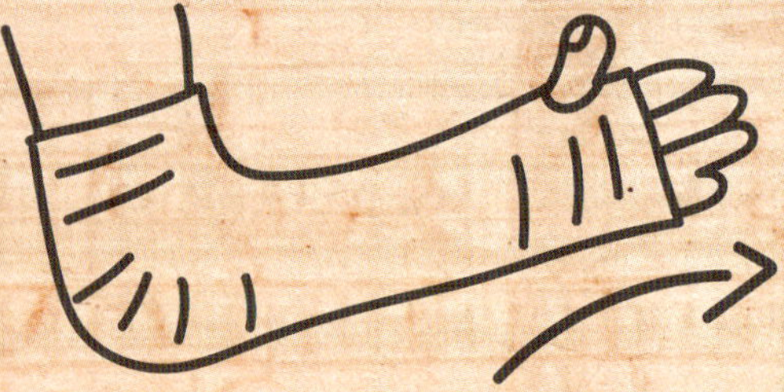

The Hawk's Nest

My next campaign is gonna be lobbying for improved OBX infrastructure. —Kiara

## Storm Drain

I like being on the water—not under it. —Kie

## Rotting Church Beams

We found the cross, though. Worth it.

## Church Steeple

Leave it to Rafe to burn up a church. See, I'm not kidding when I call my brother the Antichrist! —Sarah

OBX
SUMMER MOVIE SERIES
ADMIT ONE
61 69

MY MOVIES ARE:
1. THE OUTSIDERS
2. HEATHERS
3. THE BIG LEBOWSKI

My favorite refreshments are:
Buncha Crunch
Chili lime churros
Spiked agua fresca

My movies are:

1. Jaws
2. The Goonies
3. Weird Science

My favorite refreshments are:

Pizza

Nachos

Veggies and dip

Seriously?!
—Kie

I don't want to go into a sugar coma and fall asleep during the movie!

My favorite refreshments are:
Hot dogs
Twinkies
Any and all leftovers that Kiara can smuggle from The Wreck

My movies are:
1. Raiders of the Lost Ark
2. The Treasure of the Sierra Madre
3. Stand By Me

My movies are:
1. The Breakfast Club
2. Romancing the Stone
3. Dirty Dancing

My favorite refreshments are:
SkinnyPop, obviously
Vodka soda hidden in a Nalgene bottle
Mint chocolate chip ice cream

My movies are:

1. C.H.U.D.
2. They Live
3. Up in Smoke

Surprise, surprise.
—Kie

My favorite refreshments are:

Special brownies

Special gummies

A cold one

The kind with fruit juice, so it's nutritious.
—JJ

Remember when I lit the movie screen on fire?
—Kie

# HEYWARD'S SEAFOOD

Hurricane Agatha swooping in brought crazy times for my dad's store. Kooks placed orders for essential emergency supplies and Heyward's Seafood was happy to deliver . . . for a premium price. But I'm a little suspicious of what Kooks consider "essential."

# HEYWARD'S SEAFOOD

## PURCHASE ORDER FORM

Order for: L. Keen

Address: 1506 Vanderhorst Drive

Notes:

| ITEM | UNIT PRICE | TOTAL |
|---|---|---|
| SkinnyPop bags x 10. Note — Assorted mix, no cheddar! | | |
| Bottled spring water x 3 gallons | | |
| Martini olives x 4 | | |
| Bloody Mary mix x 3 | | |
| Liters of soda x 5. Note — DIET ONLY | | |
| Fancy Feast Gourmet Cat Food x 4. Note — ORGANIC ONLY | | |
| Bottle of cocktail sauce x 10 | | |
| Jar of cornichons x 2 | | |

Signature:

Date:

Kook family pets eat better than I do.
—JJ

Everyone eats better than you do, JJ.
—Kiara

Every summer my pop sets up a booth
at the big Boardwalk Summer Festival.
He makes a killing selling oyster
shooters to all the drunk visitors.
Boardwalk
Summer Festival
Join Us for Food • Sun • Fun
May 20th, 10 a.m. – 4 p.m.

One time The Wreck had a booth next to ours. Kiara and Sarah were still enemies, and Sarah went to order a basket of clam bellies and Kiara wouldn't even serve her. I think she said, "Traitors go hungry." So I told Sarah to come spend her money at Heyward's, and Kiara got pissed at me.

Kiara WAS kind of a bitch to me that day! I love clam bellies. —Sarah

My rage was warranted! —Kie

Then Kiara told the rest of us that Sarah was the worst person alive and we were forbidden to even go talk to her.

I'm so glad we stranded them on a boat all night long to make up. —JJ

Yeah, where would you guys even be without me? —Sarah

Even though I love the outer Banks, I can't wait to get out of here and go to college. But college is expensive and tips from shucking oysters aren't gonna cut it, so I gotta hustle another way—academics.

That noggin is firing on all cylinders. —John B

Mr. Sunn, my favorite teacher.

History teacher extraordinaire and an excellent translator of Gullah. —John B

Mine, too. Clearly. —JJ

Studying + coursework = good grades.
Good grades = college admission and scholarships.
Scholarships = my ticket out of here.
It's just a simple mathematical equation.

Studying + coursework = Laaaaame.
How's that for a math equation? —JJ

## REPORTS AND ESSAYS I WROTE FOR CLASS

Why, Pope, why? —Sarah

HONORS CHEMISTRY

Emerging Industrial Contaminants Along the North Carolina Coast

by Pope Heyward

Let's hope not . . . —Kie

ENGLISH LITERATURE

What if deserted island survival tactics come in handy one day?

Realism in Robinson Crusoe

by Pope Hey...

Science AND history? Snoozefest. —JJ

HISTORY

Medical Examinations During the Middle Ages

by Pope Heyward

PHYSICS

I remember we tested this outside your dad's store with a homemade rocket. How many windows did we accidentally break? —John B

The Effects of Launch Angle on Rocket Trajectories

by Pope Heyward

Three. The parental units were less than pleased.

I'm determined to be the first in the Heyward family to go to college. My pops likes to say college is overrated . . . but I know he's real proud of me and will rip me a new one if I mess up my prospects again. Ever since I sank my chance at the Lucas T. Vanderhorst Merit Scholarship, I've been burning the midnight oil working on my practice college admission essays.

Sank it faster than the Royal Merchant in the Great Storm. —Sarah

I, too, burn the midnight oil, if you catch my drift. —JJ

John D. Rockefeller said, "I always try to turn every disaster into an opportunity." Maybe I can do the same.

And John B Routledge supports this. Determined Pope is my favorite Pope. —John B

I can still remember the exact moment I cratered the biggest opportunity of my life. Because I chose to crater it.

I was sweating through my too large suit, sitting in a stuffy law office. It was stuffy both from the heavy North Carolina heat and from the attitude of the three fancy scholarship selection committee members I faced. They were the decision-makers on whether my year of studying and lost sleep was going to pay off. They were the arbiters of whether I would be chosen for a merit scholarship I had trained my whole academic life for. If I got this scholarship, I would be set. My parents were counting on me. I was counting on myself.

I taught Pope how to tie a tie. My little boy is growing up so fast. —JJ

But so were my friends. My group of friends is like my chosen family. We have each others' backs through it all, thick and thin. Sometimes I feel like it's us against the world. In that moment, the world was winning. A prize we had been searching for was unfairly snatched away, and it all felt like game over. Maybe every platitude I'd ever heard was wrong. Maybe working hard and showing up wasn't enough. Because when my friends needed me, I had decided to throw in the towel. And without them nothing mattered.

That's why Pogues have to stick together. —John B

But while I was sitting in that sweltering law office reciting the answers I had prepared, something dawned on me. There was one last chance to get our prize. But it could only work if my friends and I stuck together. In that moment I realized I had a choice to make, one that would define the rest of my life.

Pope chose Pogues For Life! —Kie

Opportunities come and go, but there are precious few chances to be there for your friends when it really matters. In the end, I decided to be there for them.

POPE

Heyward's Seafood also caters events around town. Whether it's a highbrow society party or lowbrow tailgate, everyone likes a seafood platter. Over the years I've seen practically every event the island has to offer.

## Daughters of the American Revolution Debutante Ball

Those people loved talking about their historical lineage almost as much as they loved shoveling down stone crab.

Why do people even like eating this? so slimy. —Sarah

## Pelican Historical Society Cotillion

Girls dancing in white dresses + platters of shrimp and pitchers of cocktail sauce = dangerous combo. More red splatters than one of JJ's slasher films. More shrieking girls too.

Is there a difference between a debutante ball and a cotillion?? —Kiara

Yes, and sadly I learned it at a very young age. Welcome to Kook life. —Sarah

## Kildare County Sheriff's Department Annual Holiday Party

Ever seen Shoupe drunk on Moscow mules, slinging back oysters, and singing a karaoke cover of "I Fought the Law" by The Clash?

I fought the law, and the law won!

It might be worth getting thrown back in the slammer just to witness that. —John B

Actually, I bet the hangover won.

## Vanderhorst Homeowners Association Annual Autumn Gala

Vanderhorst is the rich part of town, so they know how to throw a party (and pay for it). What they don't know how to do is tip or treat me and my pops like actual hardworking human beings. But we got back at them—left bags full of empty shellfish and fish bones in their garbage cans and conveniently "forgot" to tie the bags shut and close the lids. The next morning the whole street stank worse than their Kook manners. My dad never lets anyone get one over on a Heyward.

I've always wanted to be a coroner. The job requires curiosity, critical thinking, problem-solving, and attention to detail.

How did we grow up together and turn out so different?? —JJ

I'll need a background in biology, medicine, criminology, and a board certification in forensic pathology. But my pops always tells me to have a plan B . . . so just in case, sometimes I consider what else I'd like to do with my life.

Engineer: My specialty will be pulley systems designed to lower people into subterranean wells.

Surprisingly useful. —John B

Lawyer: I can try to right all the wrongs on the island and take back what belongs to The Pogues.

And you can get me out of jail easy. Just shout "objection, your honor!" —JJ

Could have come in useful for me too. —John B

We can come up with some new jobs for you, Pope. That's what friends are for, to champion your strengths. —Sarah

## PREACHER MAN

You looked pretty stately up on Denmark's pulpit. —John B

## CAR MECHANIC

You'd be in heaven working with wrenches and covered in oil stains. —JJ

## PROFESSIONAL SLEUTH

You are pretty solid at finding hidden objects and solving mysteries. —Kiara

Can you solve where my short board went? Been missing for months. —John B

## STUNT DRIVER

Inject you with some adrenaline, strap you behind the wheel, and put the pedal to the metal!. —JJ

Pope's already totaled my dad's truck. I dont think stunt driver is his calling. . . —Kiara

JJ isn't the only one who gets to have all the fun dreaming of ways to spend the $400 million.

## HOW I WOULD SPEND THE MONEY

- Top of the line research vessel with submarine to explore aquatic life.
- Most expensive video camera on the market—not ones that break upon impact!
- A mansion with a library big enough to have one of those fancy sliding ladders.
- A garage full of vintage cars to repair.
- Treat my parents to a relaxing vacation . . . but knowing my dad, he'll get bored after a couple of days and come back home to keep hustling.
- A private tutor to learn Gullah, the Creole language Denmark Tanny used to secretly communicate with his son.
- Found The Denmark and Cecilia Tanny Scholarship Foundation.
- Restore Denmark's Freedman's Assembly Church to its former glory.

*Only Pope would voluntarily give himself more homework! —Kie*

## HOW KIE WOULD SPEND THE MONEY

- Record a double album in my mansion with its own in-house studio stocked with every instrument.
- Pay for lawyers to negotiate emancipation from my parents!
- Private chef—for once I won't have to make food for other people.
- Donate to every environmental charity there is and save every animal on the endangered species list.
- Think I could buy Kildare Island and let it return to its natural state before humans polluted everything? Kick out all the residents and just let the turtles and seaweed take over.

Does Pope Heyward Esq do family law? —Kie

Since we'll each have mansions on our own private islands, sure, why not? —John B

## HOW SARAH WOULD SPEND THE MONEY

- Wardrobe makeover with haute couture. If I'm gonna get spendy, I want to do it in style.
- Wardrobe makeover for John B, because, obviously.
- Buy Tannyhill, kick out my family, hand the keys over to Pope.
- Round-the-world trip with Wheezie. Gotta get my sister out of the bubble wrap sooner or later.
- One of those private trips to space rich people take now—it's the closest I can get to the constellations. Better yet, I'll rent out the rocket for all my friends. Pogue blast-off.

Wait, I didn't agree to this! —John B

Mad respect, Sarah.

Ride the cosmic wave together. —JJ

Until I can get my share of the gold, I'll save up for the things I like to collect. Like antique electronics. I score retro tech online for dirt cheap and then try to repair it. I get to see how everything is engineered on the inside. And it's cool to hunt for something unique.

I'll stick to hunting for gold. —John B

RETRO TECH I'VE COLLECTED

- Vintage iPod: I can listen to music while studying and avoid falling into an internet rabbit hole.
- Retro '90s camcorder: RIP. Met its end when it slammed into the pavement after JJ kicked me!

Because Kiara stepped on my hand! —JJ

I was evading a murderous Ward in the rain at night! —Kie

- Gameboy: Tetris makes my brain happy.
- Polaroid camera: For taking Pogue selfies, old-school style.

Cool late 1900s technology.

Remember you found that Gameboy when I dragged you to that thrift store on the mainland two summers ago? I was looking to score some vintage vinyl records. Thrifting is like the epitome of sustainability. —Kie

Ooh, Kie, can we go vintage clothes shopping? You have the coolest threads. We'll drag with boys with us too. —Sarah

Uh I think the boys are busy that day . . . —JJ

One time I hit the jackpot when I found a science surplus company that was going out of business. I picked up a chemistry set, gear motors, anatomy figures, and more. And a bunch of posters I put up in my room, like a layout of the solar system and the Periodic Table of Elements.

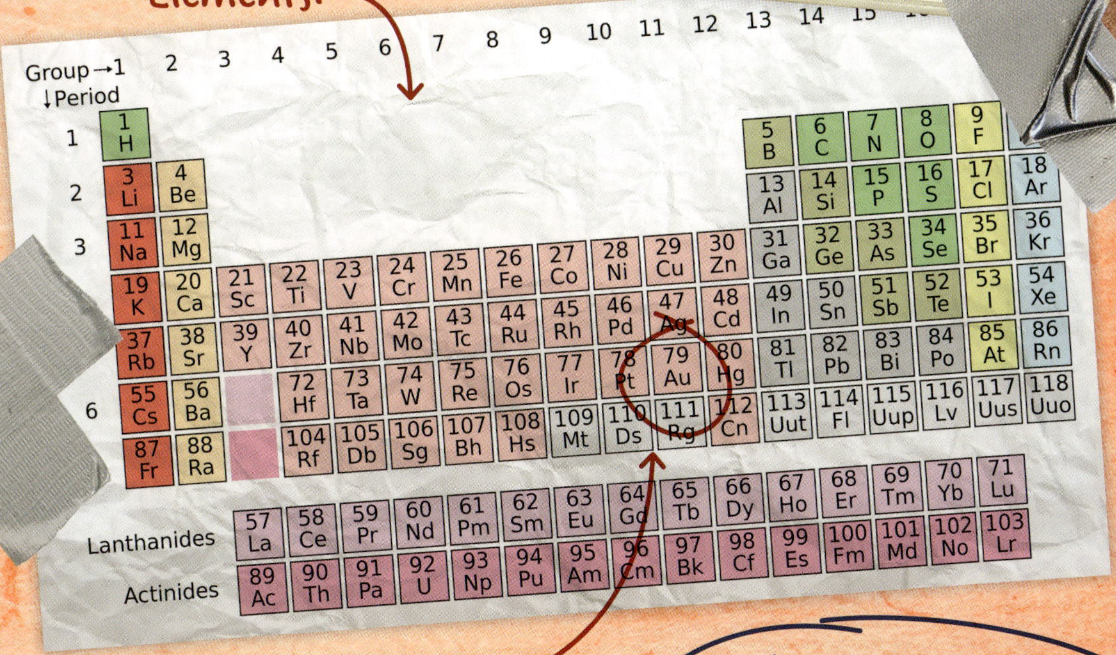


Found the gold!

*Definitive proof that Pope is Lord of the Dorks. —Kie*

It's missing the most important two letter symbol: "JJ." —JJ

# sarah

Sarah, I had my doubts when John B said you were joining the G-game. But I should know to never doubt my broski. You're pretty cool for a Kook princess, and I'm stoked you roll with us now. Even if it means I have to split my cut of the gold five ways! —JJ

If someone told me I'd make a Pogue out of Ward Cameron's daughter, I'd ask them what they were smoking and could I have some? But somehow you escaped your bubble wrap and found yourself on the wrong side of the island with me. And I found myself a whole new path with you. JB X SC. —John B

Hey, Sarah, sorry I spent two years telling everyone you were a massive bitch who can't be trusted! No hard feelings? I'm really glad the guys stranded us together to become friends again (even though it was total patriarchal bullshit!). You're one of us now, and I wouldn't have it any other way.
—Kie

Sarah, you're a Kook by birth and Pogue by heart. I'm happy you got roped into our adventure and that you're going full Pogue. I can't believe we didn't scare you off yet! You're part of our crew now, and we're better for it. —Pope

It's not every summer I fall in love, become a Pogue, realize my family are psychopaths, fake die at sea, then come back from the grave.

The Newspaper for Today's Outer Banks • Breaking News 24/7

OUTER BANKS

# Gazette

## Teens Presumed Dead at Sea

BY T. SCOTT
SENTINEL STAFF

Two Outer Banks teens are presumed dead at sea after driving their boat into the eye of a tropical storm. Sarah Cameron and John Booker Routledge were evading law enforcement when the tragedy occurred. Routledge is the primary suspect in the shooting death of Outer Banks police chief Susan Peterkin. SBI agents attempted to contact Routledge and Cameron over radio and bring them to safe

Gazette

## ed Kites Obstruct Hotel Views

ent heavy swells again

has also grown steadily, Leonard said. Th ranks increase eight woman to 13 in 201 2015-16. In ad

E. REDD | PHOTOGRAPHER

## Daughter of Local Businessman Feared Dead

BY T. SCOTT
SENTINEL STAFF

Sarah Cameron, 16, the daughter of respected Outer Banks resident and Cameron Properties founder Ward Cameron, is presumed dead after the boat she was on disappeared in the eye of last week's hurricane. She was traveling with her boyfriend, John Booker Routledge, a local teen from The Cut. Sources say Routledge brainwashed her into boarding his 858 Fantom performance speedboat and attempting to leave the island.

Coming back to the island was a total missed opportunity to pop up like a ghost and scare the shit out of people. Could you imagine the look on Rose's face?

Or Topper's. Looks like we'll have to find another way to come back from the dead and get some haunted payback.
—John B

I SURVIVED
THE GRAVEYARD
OF THE ATLANTIC
*and all I got*
*was this lousy sticker*

The boat we took to get back to OBX worked out a little better than the Fantom. When I was a girl I always dreamed I'd have a wedding under the stars . . . I guess it came true.

I guess that makes me Pogue Prince Charming.
—John B

Dude is so whipped! —JJ

"By the power vested in me by the sky, the stars, and the sea, I now pronounce us husband and wife. Through sickness and health, through rich and poor, till death do us part."

Let's not detail everything that happened that night.

Good idea! —Kie

Does this mean we get a registry and our friends will buy us things? —John B

# MY GUIDE to Sneaking Around Tannyhill

Tannyhill is like a minefield. Ward sees everything, Rose is suspicious of my every move, Rafe is always up to no good, and Wheezie always wants to know what's going on (I don't blame, her though). So I became an expert on evasive strategies in my own home.

First, listen to the grate upstairs and hear if anyone's walking around below.

If I don't go past the third step down, Ward can't see me from his office.

Beg Wheezie to snoop around to make sure the coast is clear. One day I'll return the favor and cover when she sneaks out to party and meet boys.

I never try to sneak past the sunroom when people are inside. Window exposure is too risky.

Even if I think the coast is clear, I always look up—Rose could be lurking!

Rafe could be too.

Getting outside doesn't mean I'm free. Ward likes to be the king of his castle and survey all he owns, so I stash my bicycle on the edge of the property where he can't see, and I ride off from there.

FREEDOM!

I recommend living as an unemancipated minor. It's so much easier. —John B

# Times Rafe Was the Worst

Besides when he shot me. And tried to drown me. And burned down the building I was hiding in. Okay, Rafe wasn't always such a mental case when we were younger, but we didn't exactly have a loving sibling bond . . .

- He stole money out of Ward's desk and said I took it for a shopping spree.
- One time I asked him to kill a spider in my room. He did . . . and left it on my pillow.
- He ripped apart my dollhouse and ripped the heads off the dolls.
- Once when we played hide-and-seek, he locked me in the cellar for three hours and told Rose I ran away.
- He hid his weed in Wheezie's room so Ward wouldn't find it.
- He creeped on Kiara during our sleepovers.

That was when, last year? —JJ

Very funny, J.J. I was six years old.

Major creeper. —Kie

I'd list all the times Rafe was the worst to me, but I might run out of ink . . .
—John B

- Ward was gonna gift me his old car, but one night Rafe took it for a joyride with Kelce and totaled it. So Ward used the insurance payout to lease me a brand new Volvo XC90 instead. I guess Rafe being the worst actually worked out in my favor that time.

Listening to Rafe getting in trouble yet again. You'd think he would have learned by now . . .

# Sarah and Wheezie

My sister can be annoying, and nosy, and a gossip . . . but she's the only person in my family I actually like. And obviously the only one I can trust. Wheezie can be really sweet, and I know she looks up to me and just wants to tag along.

One time I drove to Topper's for a movie night, and as soon as I parked, Wheezie popped up from the back seat. So sneaky! I didn't want to turn back, so I brought her along and she sat on the couch between us. Wheezie was in heaven.

Learning the stowaway game when she's young. Smart girl. —JJ

Wheezie ♡ Topper

# Events at the Cameron Estate

EVERYTHING OUT OF THIS MOUTH IS A LIE!

AM I IN IT FOR HIS GOLD?

Ward and Rose like to put on this perfect facade and host fancy events and act like island royalty. I think it's just an excuse to show off. I can't believe no one else sees through the bullshit.

"Kook blinders" effect. Everything looks better through the lens of money. —Pope

Literally my idea of a nightmare. —Kie

Pogues need to crash and show 'em how to really party. —JJ

*The Cameron Family*
*requests your presence for their annual*
*Backyard Ball*

WHERE: Tannyhill
WHEN: Saturday, May 25th

---

Join us for a night of music and dancing under the stars.

A silent auction will be held.

Cocktails and refreshments will be served.

PLEASE RSVP BY MAY 11TH.

# My Guide to Kook House Parties

Ward never liked letting me have parties at Tannyhill. He was so controlling. But when I was a Kook princess, my friends let me host at their places when their parents were on vacation. It wasn't summer in Figure 8 without a Sarah Cameron party.

How come I was never invited? —JJ

Uh, because fights tend to break out when you show up? —Kiara

## MY LIST OF PARTY-PLANNING ADVICE:

1) Don't invite too many people. The more exclusive it seems, the more people will show up.
2) Remove rugs and things that can break. Avoiding parental wrath is always a good idea.
3) Stock up on food and drinks. This should go without saying.
4) Bring a bathing suit. You never know when it might become a pool party.
5) Have pool flotation devices at the ready for prime social media photo opps.
6) Have a music playlist so there's never a dull moment.
7) Plug extra phone chargers around — someone's always gonna ask for one.
8) Invite old boyfriends so they can see what they're missing out on.
9) Set aside blankets for the friends who pass out and end up crashing. Gotta be a good host!
10) Make sure your friends post photos. Pics or it didn't happen.
11) Don't be afraid to call it an early night.

# A Day in the Kook Life

## JULY 2020

Life was a lot calmer before I went full Pogue!

**11th**

Saturday

10 A.M. – BEACH YOGA LED BY SURFRIDER HUGH

Relaxing workout with a view

2 P.M. – BRUNCH AT THE ISLAND CLUB WITH TOPPER

Bottomless mimosas and French toast

3:30 P.M. – SHOPPING FOR NEW SUNGLASSES WITH WHEEZIE

Wheezie always loses her sunglasses and ends up borrowing mine.

4:30 P.M. – VOLUNTEER AT KILDARE HUMANE SOCIETY.

Adorable dogs make any day better. German shepherd-golden retriever mixes are my favorite.

7 P.M. – DINNER WITH FAMILY

I can't believe we ever had normal family dinners.

10 P.M. – SLEEPOVER AT SCARLETT'S

"Sleepover" is code for "party". Scarlett's parents were never home and she threw the most epic parties.

Wow, this is really
a day in the life of
a bubble-wrap queen.
—John B

Yeah, Pogues don't even
HAVE calendars. —JJ

At least my summer days were better spent than Rafe's. When he wasn't trying to kill me and my friends, his part-time job was apparently "drug dealer." As if "full-blown psycho" wasn't already a full-time gig.

He will definitely spend it on something stupid.

What is up with Kooks and pastels? —Kie

Day drinking and getting into fights at the Island Club.

Waiting with Topper for Pogues to serve them.

At least Topper's not 100% evil. He may think Pogues were bred to mow lawns . . . but he stopped Rafe from drowning me.

I don't really get golf, but if it keeps the boys occupied for a few hours, it can't be that bad.

Uh . . . trust me. It can get bad. Next time I run into Rafe and Topper on the golf course, I'll be prepared. —Pope

| HOLE | | 2 | 3 | 4 | 5 | 6 | | | | |
|---|---|---|---|---|---|---|---|---|---|---|
| CHAMPION | 389 | 360 | 572 | 509 | 439 | 137 | 354 | 217 | 405 | |
| HDCP | 11 | 9 | 7 | 17 | 3 | 15 | 13 | 5 | 1 | |
| REGULAR | 365 | 323 | 555 | 490 | 439 | 112 | 342 | 205 | 387 | 3218 |
| HDCP | 11 | 9 | 3 | 17 | 1 | 15 | 13 | 5 | 7 | |
| PAR | 4 | 4 | 5 | 5 | 4 | 3 | 4 | 3 | 4 | 36 |
| Topper | 5 | 3 | 3 | 5 | 4 | 4 | 3 | 5 | 4 | 36 |
| Rafe | 7 | 5 | 4 | 5 | 6 | 8 | 3 | 5 | 6 | 49 |
| Kelce | 6 | 4 | 3 | 4 | 4 | 6 | 4 | 4 | 5 | 40 |
| | | | | | | | | | | |
| LADIES | 341 | 228 | 419 | 409 | 359 | 112 | 287 | 115 | 330 | 2600 |
| PAR | 4 | 4 | 5 | 5 | 4 | 3 | 4 | 3 | 4 | 36 |
| HDCP | 3 | 5 | 7 | 17 | 1 | 9 | 11 | 15 | 13 | |

Scorer:

Attest:

Date:

NSFW
—JJ

I worked as a caddy at the golf club two summers back. Management were total dicks to me. I wanted to let 'em know that, so one day at dawn I snuck John B in, and we used a rake to draw a bunch of dicks all over the sand traps. Old Kook golfers went crazy, spent the day complaining. Ah, sweet, sweet revenge. —JJ

Our work was truly an artistic masterpiece.
—John B

# Topper's Workout Journal

Why so mad, bro?
—Pope

He was so obsessive about it!

Sunday, April 12th

Plyo Push-ups – 3 sets of 20 reps
Pull-ups – 3 sets of 12 reps. Bodyweight + 20lb
V Sit-ups – 4 sets of 40 seconds work,
20 seconds rest. No pain, no gain!
Bicep Curls – 3 sets of 10 reps at 40lb
Dumbbell Row – 3 sets of 12 reps at 85lb
Personal best, heck yeah.
Hanging Oblique Crunch – 3 sets of 20 reps

Dude takes this way too seriously. Maybe he's compensating for something.
—Kiara

Topper can have all the fancy gym equipment he wants. I still got his girl.
—John B

# My Summer Volunteer Work

Just because I grew up a Kook doesn't mean I did nothing but sip spritzers on the beach all summer. I knew how privileged I was, so I always liked to give back.

Friends of Masonboro Beach

Shady Acres Nursing Home
WITH GREAT THANKS TO:
Cameron
Did you see my Meemaw there? —Pope
KILDARE COUNTY YOUTH ARTS CENTER
CERTIFIES THAT:
1
South Creek FOOD PANTRY
CONGRATULATES
Sarah Cam
If you ever catch me doing community service, I'll probably be wearing an orange jumpsuit. Just sayin'. —JJ

# Pogue Fashion

Bandana

Also makes a good wedding ring. —John B

Most important accessory. —JJ

Who needs the Sig Sauer when you've got these guns? —JJ

Sleeveless tees

Gotta add the friendship bracelet we made back into the rotation. —Kie

When you think about it, isn't clothing really just to serve as protection against the elements? Why does everyone make such a big deal about it? I guess cargo shorts are useful. —Pope

Seriously, what's the deal with the no buttons? I don't think this is what people meant when they graffitied the town with "Free John B."

I just gotta feel that sea breeze.
—John B

# Vlad and Valerie

If things get too hot on the island, Vlad and Valerie can enlist for one more top secret mission before getting out of the spy game.

Can blend in with a barbershop quartet. —John B

VLAD

Origin: Vienna

Skills:

Advanced weaponry and firearms.
Master of disguise.
Daring aquatic escapes.
Keeps calm in enclosed spaces like a well.

You mean finger guns.

Weaknesses:

Will reveal top secret objective of mission.
Unable to keep the mission strictly professional.

VALERIE

Origin: Quebec

Skills:

Fluent in six languages.
Art of seduction.
Lying to handler.
Thorough with research.

Weaknesses:

Pogue sympathizer.
Unable to keep the mission strictly professional.

# Tattoos we could get

I'm thinking we could get some ink to commemorate our good times.

Trendsetter
—JJ

I've already got a hidden dolphin tattoo.
—Kiara

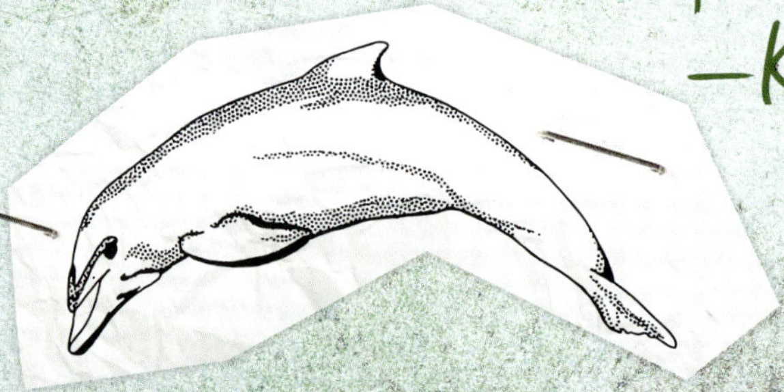

How 'bout some wheat symbol neck tats?
—John B

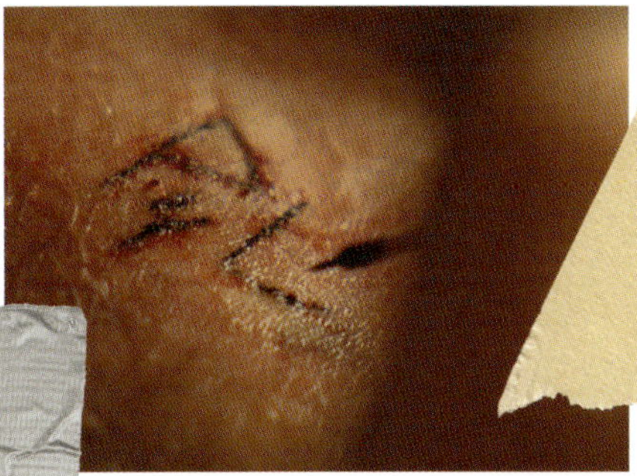

Siren of the sea to keep me company.
—JJ

How about a Denmark Tanny memorial tattoo? Gotta represent my OG Pogue ancestor. —Pope

On second thought, maybe our adventures are better remembered in our minds and over drinks at a beach bonfire. And it's not like the adventure is over . . . we've got lots more memories to make.

# OUTER BANKS - EPISODE RECAPS

## SEASON ONE

### S1, E1 PILOT

We meet the Pogues (John B, Kiara, Pope, and JJ)—a group of friends from the Outer Banks in North Carolina—and learn that John B's father has been missing for nine months. Child protective services wants to find him a foster home, a fate he avoids when a hurricane descends.

When the Pogues discover a motel room key in a sunken boat while fishing, they sneak into the motel and find contraband in a safe. JJ grabs a gun and some cash just as the cops descend, and the friends make a narrow escape. Later that night they encounter a group of Kooks—their wealthy rivals—at a beach party. A feud breaks out, and Topper—a Kook—attacks John B, nearly drowning him. JJ pulls out the gun and threatens Topper, breaking up the party.

Later the Pogues go back to the wrecked boat where they found the motel key and explore the site using scuba gear John B secretly borrowed from Ward Cameron, his boss and a powerful islander. As they leave the crash site with John B's spoils, two men in another boat try to gun them down. They make a narrow getaway due to Kiara's quick thinking. Back at shore, John B opens the bag he pulled from the wreck. Inside is his missing father's compass.

### S1, E2 THE LUCKY COMPASS

When John B drops off the scuba gear he "borrowed," he is caught by Sarah Cameron, Ward's daughter and Topper's girlfriend. Sarah agrees not to turn him in, but unfortunately her little sister is eavesdropping.

Convinced the compass and sunken boat tie back to his dad's disappearance, John B doubles down on his search for answers. He and JJ decide to start with Lana, the widow of Scooter, the last man seen with the boat, who was later discovered dead in the marsh. But when they arrive, Lana is being threatened by the guys who tried to gun them down. After the men leave, Lana warns them to stop asking questions. Meanwhile, Wheezie (Sarah's little sister) rats out John B for taking the scuba gear. John B is consequently fired by Ward.

Back at home, John B opens his father's compass and finds the word "Redfield" carved into it. Then the two goons who threatened Lana show up looking for the compass, and the Pogues hide as the goons raid John B's father's office and take his research into the *Royal Merchant*, a ship that sank with millions of dollars of gold on board and was never found. When the coast is clear, the Pogues go to the Redfield lighthouse. John B is desperate for answers but finds none, and he impulsively kisses Kiara, who reminds him that Pogues don't hook up with each other. The goons chase John B again and John B is nearly electrocuted.

John B gives the compass to Sheriff Peterkin. Then he realizes there's a Redfield in his lineage. The message from his father was a name. John B, Kiara, JJ, and Pope drive out to John B's great-grandmother's mausoleum, where Kiara wedges herself through a gap in the door and makes a shocking discovery.

## S1, E3
## THE FORBIDDEN ZONE

The object Kiara finds in the mausoleum is an envelope containing a map showing the location of the *Royal Merchant* wreck, along with a mini-cassette recorder.

The recording is a message from John B's dad, telling John B to finish what he started. The Pogues are excited at the prospect of finding the 400-million-dollar bounty.

Rafe, Sarah Cameron's brother, makes a deal with a drug dealer named Barry to sell drugs at Topper's house party that night.

Back to the Pogues, who are seeking out ways to explore the *Royal Merchant* wreck. They eventually steal a drone. While Pope delivers groceries on Figure 8, the wealthy part of the island, Rafe and Topper jump Pope. In retaliation, Pope pulls the plug on Topper's boat, and it sinks.

The next day the Pogues go out with the drone and locate the *Royal Merchant*, which is about 1,000 feet down.

## S1, E4 SPY GAMES

The group explores the wreck for gold and comes up empty. When John B gets home, DCS is there waiting to take him to a foster home. John B runs away and encounters Sarah Cameron, who brings him to Tannyhill, her home.

John B notices a painting of Denmark Tanny, a formerly enslaved person who bought his freedom with gold and built Tannyhill estate. John B remembers Tanny survived the *Merchant* wreck and asks Sarah to get him access to the archives—which contain Tanny's letters—at UNC. In Chapel Hill, sparks fly between John B and Sarah.

Meanwhile, JJ, Pope, and Kiara go to a movie and run into Topper and Rafe. A fight breaks out between both groups until Kiara causes a distraction by setting fire to the movie screen. When Topper's family presses charges against Pope for the boat incident, JJ takes the fall and turns himself in.

## S1, E5 MIDSUMMERS

JJ's dad, Luke, bails him out of jail and then beats him. When Luke passes out, JJ points the gun at his dad's head, but can't bring himself to pull the trigger.

John B asks his high school teacher to translate a letter found in the archives and written in Gullah by Denmark Tanny. It contains a note to "harvest the wheat near the water

in parcel nine forthwith" along with a wheat symbol John B has seen in illustrations of the *Royal Merchant*'s gold.

That night, the Midsummer party at the Island Club is about to begin. Sarah doesn't want to go—she wants to break up with Topper—but Ward convinces her to attend. At the party she and John B arrange a clandestine meeting, during which John B asks her to bring him a map of Tannyhill.

Back at their hangout spot, John B fills the Pogues in on the treasure hunt and Kiara warns him to stay away from Sarah.

Sarah finds the map of Tannyhill in her father's home office, but Ward catches her. When she leaves to meet John B, Ward opens a secret safe and takes out the compass. For the first time we realize that Ward is connected to the missing gold and Big John's disappearance.

John B and Sarah meet at a lookout tower. Topper, drunk, follows Sarah and pushes John B off a railing. John B wakes up in the hospital with a concussion and a broken wrist, and Ward offers to be his legal guardian as a thank you for protecting his daughter.

## S1, E6 PARCEL 9

John B is now living at Tannyhill, unaware of Ward's machinations.

The Pogues and Sarah determine "parcel 9" is located at the property of a creepy old lady who, legend has it, murdered her husband with an axe. But that doesn't stop the Pogues from plotting to sneak into her basement to search for the gold. There's one problem—Kiara isn't comfortable with Sarah tagging along.

Kiara explains that she and Sarah used to be friends until Sarah abruptly ended things. John B refuses to choose between them, and the boys encourage a reconciliation between the girls by leaving them on a boat overnight. Sarah and Kiara resolve their issues and cautiously become friends again.

Finally the Pogues and Sarah break into the Crain house and hunt for gold. The old lady wakes up and chases them out . . . but not before John B rappels into a well. As they race from the house, John B reveals a muddy gold bar in his grasp—they found the treasure!

## S1, E7 DEAD CALM

Ward eavesdrops on John B and Sarah discussing the gold. The Pogues melt down the gold so they can pawn it but are held at gunpoint by Barry the drug dealer. The Pogues fight back, and JJ steals $25,000 from him, intending to pay off the debt for sinking Topper's boat. He and his dad fight over the money, and JJ impulsively uses the money to buy a hot tub.

Topper and Rafe confront John B and Sarah over the stolen money. Then John B takes Sarah to his special spot in the bell tower of the old church, and they sleep together for the first time. The next morning, John B and Ward wake up early to go fishing, and Ward brings up the gold. John B denies they found it, but Ward rattles off all the other things he knows—like the Redfield clue. John B realizes Ward had something to do with Big John's disappearance. As John turns back to shore intending to call the police, Ward approaches him menacingly with a gaff hook.

## S1, E8 THE RUNWAY

Ward chases John B through the boat, but John B escapes. Then Ward stabs himself with a speargun and goes to the sheriff, claiming John B attacked him. John B goes to Lana (Scooter's wife), who tells him the truth about the night his dad disappeared.

Big John and Ward had begun working together to find the *Royal Merchant*, and Big John had found it—but they disagreed about how to split the profits. They fought, and Big John hit his head on a metal rope cleat. Instead of calling for help, Ward stole Big John's map, pushed his body overboard, and sank the boat.

John B, furious, grabs the gun JJ stole. He sneaks into Sarah's room to tell her what happened, but she doesn't believe him. John B goes back to the well to get the rest of the gold, but Ward got there first. All the gold is gone.

Pope blows an important scholarship interview the next morning after learning Ward Cameron hired a plane to transport heavy cargo. Pope knows it can only mean one thing—that Ward plans to fly the gold off the island.

On the airport tarmac, Ward tries to force Sarah onto the plane with him to the Bahamas, and John B intervenes. He drives their VW bus—the Twinkie—onto the runway to block the plane's takeoff, and Sheriff Peterkin arrives to make an arrest . . . but it's not John B, it's Ward. He's under arrest for the murder of John Routledge. Suddenly a gunshot rings out. Rafe steps out with a gun, and the sheriff falls to the ground, bleeding.

## S1, E9 THE BELL TOWER

Sheriff Peterkin, dying, urges John B to flee the scene while Ward sends the plane on to the Bahamas with the gold. Ward blames the murder of Sheriff Peterkin on John B in order to protect Rafe. He locks Sarah in her room to prevent her from exposing the truth, but Sarah eventually escapes with her sister's help and finds John B, who is now on the run. The other Pogues attempt to protect them while the police lead a manhunt for John B. At the height of the drama, Pope professes his love to Kiara but gets his heart broken. As John B and Sarah continue to evade authorities, Topper discovers their hiding spot and alerts the police. Rafe sets their hiding place on fire in an effort to smoke them out, but Topper tries to prove his love for Sarah by tricking the police so she and John B can escape.

## S1, E10 THE PHANTOM

A tropical storm begins to gather, and the manhunt gains steam. Ward stops Sarah before she can tell the authorities what really happened on the tarmac. JJ steals the keys to his father's speedboat, and John B returns home for the nugget of gold he has stashed there. As the Pogues retrieve the boat, Rafe and Barry arrive and fight them. It ends with Pope beating and nearly strangling Rafe.

John B meets up with the Pogues, and Sarah decides to escape with him. They are soon spotted when power is restored to the city's lighthouse, which illuminates them in the bay. The authorities give chase, forcing John B and Sarah into the middle of the storm. Ward attempts via radio to convince John B to bring Sarah back. John B then reveals Ward's crimes over the radio. John B and Sarah decide to press through the storm, but they capsize and their radio dies. John B and Sarah are presumed dead. Unbeknownst to the other Pogues, John B and Sarah managed to survive the storm. Stranded in the open sea, they use the gold nugget as a signal beacon and are rescued by a cargo ship on its way to the Bahamas. They now have a chance to recover the gold.

# SEASON TWO

## S2, E1 THE GOLD

JJ, Kiara, and Pope grieve while the rest of the community gathers to honor Sheriff Peterkin.

But John B and Sarah are alive on a cargo ship headed for the Bahamas. The ship's crew learns there's a $50,000 reward for their capture and Terrence, the ship's captain, wants that money. He plans to turn them over to the police as soon as they dock in Nassau . . . but John B and Sarah escape. John B sends a text from a borrowed cell phone, alerting the Pogues that he and Sarah are alive. Then he breaks into the Camerons' Bahamas home but fails to crack the code to the safe where the gold is stored. Sarah gets kidnapped by Terrence, but John B and Sarah strike a bargain: they'll team up with Terrence and his crew to steal the rest of the gold. Meanwhile, Pope, Kiara, and JJ plot to clear John B's name. Pope wiretaps a conversation between Ward and his pilot Gavin, who still has the murder weapon from the tarmac and is blackmailing Ward.

In the Bahamas John B, Sarah, and Terrence's crew sneak back into the Cameron home. They open the safe, but the security system alerts Ward, and security guards arrive. Terrence and his crew escape, but John B is apprehended. Ward tells the guards to show him the culprit's face . . .

## S2, E2 THE HEIST

. . . but Sarah sabotages security's plans for John B, and they both make a run for it before security can reveal John B's identity.

Back in the Outer Banks, Pope, Kiara, and JJ secretly film a meeting between Ward and Gavin. It ends with Ward shooting Gavin in cold blood, then losing the murder weapon

in a storm drain. An angry Kiara saw the whole thing and inadvertently draws Ward's attention. Ward chases the Pogues away, causing Pope to drop his video camera and ruin the footage.

Ward cleans up his mess with Rafe's help, and Rafe is determined to retrieve the gun. But Kiara manages to get to it first. The Pogues give it to Deputy Shoupe as evidence, but he still doesn't believe their tale.

In the Bahamas John B, Sarah, Terrence, and Terrence's crew enact their plan to intercept the gold before Ward transports it. Ward and Rafe arrive in the Bahamas, and a car chase ends with Ward seeing that the robbers are none other than John B and Sarah—his own daughter—who is alive! Rafe tries to shoot John B but accidentally hits Sarah.

## S2, E3 PRAYERS

John B leaves the gold behind and races to find a doctor to save Sarah's life, intending to meet up with Terrence and Cleo on a boat with the gold as soon as she's better. As the doctor operates, Sarah's condition seemingly deteriorates . . . until she makes a surprise recovery.

In the Outer Banks: Pope receives a mysterious letter from "C. Limbrey." It claims to have evidence that can exonerate John B.

Pope, JJ, and Kiara prep for a trip to Charleston to retrieve C. Limbrey's supposed evidence.

John B and a weakened Sarah rush to the dock to meet Terrence . . . but they're too late. Ward recovered the gold. Sarah is tired of running and wants to go back home to clear John B's name. They begin the journey back by boat, declaring themselves married along the way.

## S2, E4 HOMECOMING

John B and Sarah stop in Charleston to refuel en route to OBX. Meanwhile, Pope meets with Carla Limbrey, another person Ward teamed up with to hunt for gold, and later double-crossed. She thinks Pope's family has a special key, but Pope has no knowledge of a key. JJ and Kiara show up just in time to save Pope from Carla's henchman and half-sibling, Renfield. As they escape through the streets of Charleston, they intercept John B and Sarah. It's an epic reunion. The friends return to the Outer Banks.

The Pogues celebrate, and Pope and Kiara sneak off to hook up. Rafe and Barry crash the party—looking to kill John B—but John B, JJ, and Sarah manage to evade them. Sarah returns home and urges Ward to make Rafe turn himself in. Ward refuses. He calls the police, who follow Sarah back to the Pogues. John B is forced to surrender.

## S2, E5 THE DARKEST HOUR

John B is charged with murder. Pope sets out to discover more about the Tanny key and learns his great-grandmother used to wear it around her neck. He searches her old apartment and matches a ceiling pattern to the pattern in a drawing Limbrey gave him . . . which leads him to find the key! It is inscribed with a cryptic message: "The path to the tomb begins in the Island Room."

Meanwhile Ward pays off a police officer, who releases a murderous inmate to strangle John B, but John B fights him off. Rafe tricks Sarah into meeting him under the guise of meeting Wheezie.

JJ tries to break John B out of jail by means of an elaborate plan involving a stolen ambulance. The plan fails and nearly gets him arrested.

When Sarah shows up to meet "Wheezie," Rafe tries to drown her, but Topper saves her.

Meanwhile, Deputy Shoupe receives a ballistics report with evidence linking the gun—which the Pogues handed over—to Rafe. Shoupe and other officers descend on Tannyhill to arrest Rafe for murder.

## S2, E6 MY DRUTHERS

John B is released from prison and retrieves his beloved van, the Twinkie. He returns to the Chateau for a joyful reunion with his friends. Sarah shows up with Topper, who can't help but stick it to John B: he was there for Sarah when John B wasn't. Meanwhile, Kiara tells Pope she doesn't want a relationship.

Pope visits his great-grandmother in the nursing home. She tells Pope they are direct descendants of Denmark Tanny.

Limbrey and Renfield—determined to get the key—demand the key in exchange for a voice recording containing damning evidence against Ward. Pope trades the key, but John B and JJ had swapped it out for a different antique key. The Pogues deliver the recording to Shoupe, who finally realizes they've been telling the truth about Ward.

Ward finds Rafe and plots to get him off the island, but Barry betrays him, and Rafe is arrested. Law enforcement moves to arrest Ward, and the Pogues rush to Tannyhill to watch. Ward, aboard the *My Druthers*, has anchored just off the dock. Sarah pleads with Ward not to leave. It's too late; Ward blows up the boat and himself along with it.

## S2, E7 THE BONFIRE

The Cameron family grieves Ward's death. Ward left a parting video message for his family, wherein he confesses to killing Big John and Gavin, and takes the fall for murdering Sheriff Peterkin so that Rafe can go free. Rafe wants to make amends with Sarah, but she can't accept it. Sarah, upset by John B's pleased reaction to her father's death, breaks up with

John B. She turns to Topper for comfort.

Limbrey figures out the Pogues gave her the wrong key. Meanwhile, in history class, the Pogues learn that their teacher has access to the maritime museum's archives and Denmark Tanny's diary. The diary reveals that the Cross of Santo Domingo was on the *Royal Merchant*. This is what Limbrey is after.

That night, the Pogues head to a big bonfire where the Kooks are all hanging, including Sarah with Topper. A misunderstanding between Sarah and John B leads to a brawl between the Kooks and Pogues.

Later at the Chateau, Renfield forces the Pogues to hand over the real key. Limbrey then shows up at Tannyhill seeking the Island Room. The next morning, Sarah finds that the wallpaper has been torn down to reveal a hidden mural of the island.

## S2, E8 THE CROSS

Sarah informs Pope she's found the Island Room.

She brings the Pogues to Tannyhill and reveals the enormous mural. Pope remembers Denmark's last words: "You'll find the real treasure at the foot of the angel." The Pogues examine the mural, and JJ recognizes a massive tree, "Angel Oak," at the very tip of Kildare Island. The tree appears to contain a knothole on its trunk that's shaped like a keyhole. The Pogues navigate the Twinkie across a narrow land bridge; it's partially underwater during high tide.

They continue their journey on foot, finally arriving at the massive Angel Oak. They spy Rafe, Limbrey, and Renfield, who have beaten them there. The Pogues watch from their hiding place as the villains excavate a casket: the final resting place of Denmark Tanny's wife, Cecilia—his "real treasure." After Limbrey and the others leave, Pope reburies Cecilia's remains, and JJ finds the knot hole he saw in the mural. He pulls out an old spyglass. Its inscription sends the Pogues toward an old church on the mainland; but by now the tide is covering the land bridge on the peninsula and the Twinkie gets stuck.

Kiara and JJ set off to get supplies to save the Twinkie. They are intercepted by JJ's

father (Luke), who is hiding from the police and needs to get off the island. Even as the sea water threatens to consume the Twinkie, JJ can't say no to Luke. JJ helps his father leave the island for good.

Back at the submerged land bridge, John B, Pope, and Sarah are trying to save the Twinkie. An alligator surfaces and attacks John B. Sarah heroically saves him with a knife, and it brings them one step closer to reconciling.

The Pogues free the Twinkie and set off for the church, where Pope discovers the Cross of Santo Domingo high in the rafters. When Pope tries to extract the cross, he upsets a wasp nest and is attacked. He falls, lands safely, then looks upward to see the enormous cross falling forward . . .

## S2, E9 TRAPPED

The massive cross crashes to the ground, barely missing Pope, who rolls to safety just in time, but goes into anaphylactic shock from the wasp stings. The Pogues go to JJ's cousin Ricky, an EMT, for help; he administers epinephrine and saves Pope's life.

Rafe and Limbrey take the cross, having tracked Sarah's cell phone to the church, and it's gone by the time the Pogues return. Limbrey uses Tanny's key to open the cross and claim the holy garment that she thinks will cure her. Unfortunately, it's been eaten by moths. Renfield tries to steal the cross for himself, but Limbrey kills him and Rafe takes the cross.

The Pogues go to Tannyhill, where they find Rafe's truck. Before Sarah confronts Rafe, she and John B make up. Sarah takes Rafe's keys and discovers Renfield's dead body inside the truck. Rafe overpowers her and locks her in the wine cellar, where her stepmother Rose drugs her.

Rafe dumps Renfield's body in the swamp for gator feed. Then he and Pope, who followed him, brawl. Rafe gets his gun; but Pope manages to hide.

The Pogues reconnect at a shipping yard and watch as the cross is loaded onto a container ship named *The Coastal Venture*. They see Rose escorting Wheezie and a drugged Sarah on board. Pope creates a diversion and the Pogues sneak into a shipping container, which gets loaded onto the boat. When Sarah comes to, she tries to escape the room she's been locked in, but comes face-to-face with her father when she opens the door. Ward is alive!

## S2, E10 THE COASTAL VENTURE

Ward tells Sarah how he faked his own death, and says he gave John B the cross in exchange for John B staying away from Sarah. She doesn't know what to believe until she sneaks out of her room and sees that the cross is actually onboard—Ward was lying. Sarah tries to radio the coast guard but is caught by the ship's captain.

Having escaped the shipping container, the Pogues hatch a plan to take over the ship. John B is attacked by a crew member before he can secure any weapons. Pope meets Cleo—formerly of Terrence's crew in the Bahamas—in the engine room. She decides to hide the Pogues from the crew.

JJ and Kiara lock the crew below deck while John B searches for Sarah but encounters Rafe instead. Rafe and John B face off in an epic fight until a boiler explodes, helping John B escape.

Cleo helps Pope tie up the captain, and Pope tries to load the cross into a lifeboat. As Sarah climbs aboard a lifeboat, Ward confronts her, nearly strangling her until John B steps in. John B and Ward fight, and Ward hits his head, mirroring the original fight between Ward and Big John. John B finally has a chance to avenge his father's death, but he shows mercy and lets Ward live. John B and Sarah get into a lifeboat to escape.

On the other side of the ship, JJ is knocked overboard as he and Kiara battle the boat's captain, and Kiara jumps in after him. Pope struggles with the cross as the crew opens fire. He decides if he can't have the cross, no one can, and he releases the cross into the ocean. Pope and Cleo jump overboard and are rescued by John B and Sarah. Rafe and the crew pull the sinking cross back aboard the ship, and Rafe promises Ward he'll get Sarah back.

The Pogues (plus Cleo) rescue JJ and Kiara, and they all speed away in a lifeboat. They land on a deserted beach. They may not have the treasure, but they have each other.

The season ends in Barbados, where it is revealed that Big John is still alive.